Anonymous

Notes for a Memoir on the Pathology of the Teeth

Anatiposi

Anonymous

Notes for a Memoir on the Pathology of the Teeth

Reprint of the original, first published in 1871.

1st Edition 2023 | ISBN: 978-3-38211-588-3

Anatiposi Verlag is an imprint of Outlook Verlagsgesellschaft mbH.

Verlag (Publisher): Outlook Verlag GmbH, Zeilweg 44, 60439 Frankfurt, Deutschland
Vertretungsberechtigt (Authorized to represent): E. Roepke, Zeilweg 44, 60439 Frankfurt, Deutschland
Druck (Print): Books on Demand GmbH, In de Tarpen 42, 22848 Norderstedt, Deutschland

NOTES FOR A MEMOIR

ON THE

PATHOLOGY OF THE TEETH.

BY

READ BEFORE THE FIRST DISTRICT DENTAL SOCIETY OF NEW YORK.

FROM THE "DENTAL COSMOS."

PHILADELPHIA:
SAMUEL S. WHITE.
1871.

TO

TIMOTHY M. CHEESMAN, M.D.,

THESE ESSAYS

Are Inscribed,

AS A SLIGHT MARK OF RESPECT

ENTERTAINED FOR HIS CHARACTER AND TALENTS,

AND AFFECTIONATE RECOLLECTIONS OF HIS MEMORABLE FATHER,

THE AUTHOR'S PRECEPTOR,

THE LATE DISTINGUISHED PHYSICIAN AND EMINENT SURGEON,

JOHN C. CHEESMAN, M.D.,

BY

A. C. CASTLE, M.D.

PREFACE.

THE following essays, published as a serial in the DENTAL COSMOS, having elicited much attention, the author presents them to the medical and dental professions in consecutive form, hoping that the information they convey may prove acceptable. These NOTES FOR A MEMOIR ON THE PATHOLOGY OF THE TEETH are the results of many years' reflection, based upon professional practice and observation of forty years' experience. The effort has been entirely a labor of love, influenced by the desire of forming a correct basis for investigating the pathological character of the dental system, with the view of arriving at a scientific mode of treatment—apart from *mechanical* expedients and appliances only—for the preservation of the dental organs to their natural period of existence. My efforts towards this end were appreciated and encouraged by my medical preceptor, and his and my personal friend, the highly respected and distinguished physician, Francis U. Johnson, M.D.

The illustrations which embellish this work are true to nature, and exhibit the various neuralgic-sympathetic affections produced by diseases of the dental organs.

A. C. CASTLE, M.D.

NEW YORK, July 1, 1871.

NOTES FOR A MEMOIR

PATHOLOGY OF THE TEETH.

MR. PRESIDENT AND GENTLEMEN,—A few evenings since, at a meeting of this society, a gentleman made the positive assertion that when carious teeth were properly filled, as he filled them, they would endure forever. An important *desideratum*, if true. The object, then, of discussing the anatomical character, the physiological intention, and the pathological condition of the dental system, claims our attention, to the end of ascertaining whether the dental organs possess a pathology or not, or how far the thirty years' experience of the impercipient faculties of this gentleman's assertion can be sustained ; while it is the province of these notes for a memoir on the pathology of the teeth to demonstrate that the dental system holds pathological communion with the whole body, and that medicine possesses the power of reaching the abnormal changes in dental disease.

Medical history has among its records that "once upon a time" "charms" were chiefly relied upon for removing disease. After charms simple remedies were resorted to, and to these remedial agents *chance* and *experience* added vegetable and mineral poisons. "Wherefore," asked Pliny, "has our mother earth brought forth so many poisons, but that when we are wearied with suffering we may employ them for suicide?" The savage Carib and still more savage Boschman reason differently : they believe that poisons were sent to them for the destruction of their enemies ; while the believers in an overseeing Providence assume that the beneficence of the Creator sent all things into the world not for the destruction, but for the benefit of his creation.

The history of the dentist's art furnishes us with a similar sequence. First "charms" were relied upon for the cure of dental ills—the toothache ; then simple remedies were resorted to, and then followed poisons, vegetable and mineral ; and then came the dental savage, who does not assume that the beneficence of the Creator made these organs for a special purpose, but who extracts from the jaws the whole dental family, thereby removing all pathological anomalies by substituting what he terms "an artificial denture," which I presume is meant and intended for artificial *denticulation*. There are many others, however, whose rational philosophy and purer motives,—believing in the beneficent intention of nature,—make them hesitate before they destroy the design and the purpose of the dental organs. In this rational philosophy true wisdom, true science, and true art unite in supporting each other against the irrational conclusions of mere babblers.

"Ask what I shall give," said the Lord to the dreaming monarch. "An understanding heart to discern judgment," was his simple, modest request. The spirit of inquiry has an honest reverence for truth, and a profound contempt for all that is false and for all that is factitious. By the light of scientific progress the searcher after knowledge discovers many things, while at the same time he finds that there is an inner temple of mystery into which the human mind cannot enter. Let us beware how we commit ourselves. This caution especially affects those who have not deemed it to be their first duty to examine into the natural laws bearing in their regular order, whether in health or disease, upon the economy of the animal system.

If the assertion be correct that when teeth are properly filled they will endure forever, the task of discussing the pathology of the teeth, or indeed any other dental subject, is entirely useless and altogether unnecessary; for here we are told, *in fact*, that the teeth are simply an inert, incorruptible mechanical substance, which, by a mechanical addition, can be rendered durable forever. The cause of decay, however, is the first obstacle encountered, and presents a curious anomaly— the teeth can be rendered perfect while they are imperfect. The replacing by an amalgam or gold filling the decayed lost substance of the dental organs, will secure them from offending ever after, and will make them endure forever—a happy consummation devoutly to be wished for; the mere ideal of which at once suggests a happy thought. Would not the making holes into the dental organs, and properly filling the said holes with amalgam or gold, not only serve as a prophylactic against decay, but at the same time preserve the glory of the dentist's art forever?

At the present moment the science of the dentist's art is in a state of transition from its embryonic condition to its gradual development, and if to serve this end, multiplicity of teachers, boldness of speculation, and profundity of theory were all that were necessary to illuminate any subject so that the understanding might comprehend it with the least possible exertion of its powers, then, unquestionably, dental pathology, in all its aspects, should stand as clearly revealed as the sun in the heavens. But, unfortunately, a multitude of words does not always enlarge the boundaries of knowledge; and abstract theories, however ingenious, are rarely more substantial than the pasteboard architecture of our childhood.

Wishing to treat this subject with the seriousness it demands, I should be sorry to utter one word of reflection upon the elaborated chemical and microscopical analyses of the teeth "after" Berzelius, Hunter, and others,—the admirable efforts made to show that they are part and parcel of the osseous system; and, on the other hand, that they are only extraneous matter, deposited as mere mechanical instruments in the maxillary bones, and enjoying a democratic independence, free from all sympathy with the several systems, forming together one harmonious whole, which the philosophic prince so eloquently apostrophized: "What a piece of work is man!" But from my point of view my humble opinion is that writers on the pathology of the teeth have, in general, been more learned than accurate; more ingenious than practical; and following in a *beaten* track of mere speculation, they have constructed a very elegant "system," which wants only one thing to make it perfect, and that is simply a foundation in nature. These writers have altogether overlooked *constitutional peculiarities;* and, while they have gone on analyzing the substance of the teeth with the greatest patience and care, regardless of the constitutional character of the various teeth, they have left almost wholly out of view the exciting causes of nervous and organic, and the chemico-mechanical, influences produced upon them by various external and internal agencies. This error, thus stated in broad and general terms, has almost uniformly characterized the literature and the scientific discussions and debates upon the diseases of the teeth. Thus we have had presented to us an unmeaning pathology, based upon mere abstract speculations, while the *diathesis* or peculiar constitutional habit of body of each and every individual has been entirely lost sight of, though practical experience teaches and observation demonstrates to us that *there, and there alone,* can we discern the causes of each pathological condition, and of the numerous abnormal formations and secretions, as well as the many variations in the organization, ossification, and densities of the different teeth. Variations and conditions so marked and adverse that, while one individual may triturate glass with his teeth, another is subjected to excruciating torture by the mere touch of the finger-nail or a quill toothpick; such remarkable structural difference exercising, of course, peculiar influence upon the physical appearance, as well as upon the healthfulness, usefulness, and permanent durability of these organs.

As you all well know, the teeth are bones of peculiar structure, and constitute a portion of the osseous system; their component parts are similar to the other bones; but as they are intended for purposes requiring and resisting mechanical friction, their relative proportions of constituents are considerably altered to secure to them denseness, hardness, and strength. We therefore find that the inorganic or earthy matter is in increased proportion, while the crowns and necks constituting the body of the teeth are covered and protected by a hard, crystallized enamel, which, in a modified crusta petrosa, terminates on their necks and fangs.

To give vital susceptibility apart from their original uses in assisting their organization, the teeth are supplied with filaments or twigs from the grand sensitive nerve of the face and motor nerve of the jaws,—the fifth pair of nerves; this pair of nerves anastomosing with the seventh pair of nerves forming the *respiratory* nerves and those of expression of the face. The twigs of the fifth pair of nerves, entering the foramina or small holes at the end of the fangs, gradually enlarge with the dental tube until they terminate in ganglionary " pulps" in the chambers of the teeth. Entering with each twig is a complete vascular supply of arteries, veins, and absorbents, which spread over a delicate membrane lining the dento-nerve canals and chambers within the teeth. These nourish and give sensibility to the substance, while in old age we find them secreting and depositing dentine within the nerve canals, and by obliterating the nerves, devitalizing the bone of the teeth, by filling in and solidifying each tooth severally into one mass.

By this elaborate organization, and their direct connection with the grand nerves of sensibility, respiration, and expression of the jaws and face, do they not afford us ample evidence that the dental system is in harmony with pathological sympathies with every organ of the body? Yet we are told that a plug of gold in a hollowed tooth will preserve it forever.

Is it not singular, after hundreds of years' experience, that up to this moment physicians, surgeons, oculists, nor dentists have ever suspected, or if they have suspected, they have never applied their understanding to investigate and demonstrate, the pathological-sympathetic affections of the dental system with the other organs? They know that earache is sympathetic with diseased teeth. It is a popular idea, but it has no foundation in fact, that the "eye teeth" are in direct connection with the organs of vision; but, the irritation of the dental nerves, singly or generally, by dento-pathological sympathy, does superinduce *muscæ volitantes*, or motes or cobwebs, or small rings and minute disks, to float before the eye and impede the vision; that strabismus, and pains in the dense fibrous sac containing the humors and forming the eyeball, are frequent sympathetic affections of dento-neuralgic irritation; that the same nervous sympathetic influence acts upon the epiglottis and windpipe, causing spasmodic coughs and pseudo or false croup, symptoms in teething children. It also affects the organs of respiration in grown persons; and many an individual has been cured of consumptive symptoms, either by a medical attendant or some quack medicine, when the dentist should have received all the credit for his perfect treatment of the teeth, although in a state of happy innocence of his own doings, or of the sympathetic nervous irritations often affecting the dental and the respiratory systems. These are but a few of the instances offering sufficient illustration of dento-neuralgic influence upon the various organs.

By the following table of analysis of the comparative divisional components, the one of the three parts exhibits a large excess of gelatinous tissue in the *crusta petrosa*, for the purpose, no doubt, of being the medium of directly supplying the teeth, externally, with the vitalizing influence and protection of the maxillary alveoli periosteum :

LASSAIGNE'S ANALYSIS.

	Bone.	Enamel.	Crusta Petrosa.
Phosphate of lime with fluoride of calcium...	67·54	81·63	53·84
Carbonate of lime	7·97	8·83	3·98
Phosphate of magnesia	2·49	2·55	....
Soluble salts	1·00	0·97	....
Gelatin tissue	20·42	5·97	42·18
Fat	0·58	....	....
	100 00	100·00	100 00

It will be observed that over fifty per cent. of the *crusta petrosa*, forming the connection of the softer bone with the investing *periosteum* covering the fangs, is of gelatinous tissue, which, as we shall hereafter show, plays an important part in the pathology of the teeth.

By way of episode or parenthesis, I may here be permitted to say that, while "man proposes, God disposes," or in other words, Nature is our best friend ; that she acts for us as honestly as she can, and that she does not find her account in causing or prolonging disease ; that she adopts her *own* time, her own means of *vitality*, and her own plan, by her own immutable laws, to develop her work. We may force her, but we cannot control or alter her laws ; we may medicate, we may feed by the mysteries of "chemically prepared food," "rational (?) food," phosphatic medico-scientific nutrition ; yet all our appliances made to reach the goal of our intentions may be summed up in the stereotyped medical axiom, "*Improve the general health ;*" and ever-beneficient Nature and her laws are left in silence to accomplish the rest.

At the infantile period, when the greatest mobility of the organization exists, the animal economy avails itself of the nutritive material furnished, first from the maternal milk, and afterward from more solid food ; and, notwithstanding that both the milk and the solid food contain all the necessary elements for the perfect development of bones, sinews, ligaments, and muscles, we find that the periodic action of nature's laws cannot be forced nor changed. Thus we find that, from the commencement, and throughout the whole period of the primary dentition, while the first or milk teeth are being formed of corpuscular and molecular soft gelatinous predominance, the *same nutrition* is depositing an entirely different molecular arrangement of solid, dense bone basis for the formation of the permanent teeth *immediately behind* the deciduous teeth. We might ask why the milk teeth do not partake of the better nutrition; but we find the very opposite; and, absolutely, while nutrition is forwarding the completion of the permanent, the dental absorbents are actually sucking away and removing the temporary teeth, and, for aught we know to the contrary, the absorption of the molecules of the one giving its particles of nutrition to the other.

I would call your attention to the fact that the formation of the teeth, in the second dentition, is at that period-time of the animal formation, as a general rule, when the digestive organs are in good condition, and when assimilation and nutrition bear with all the vigor of the vital forces on the animal economy for the perfect development of the being. This process we find to be in harmony with the peculiar constitution of each several individual; and, in accordance with the constitutional organization, the teeth present no better construction, and they are of *no higher* grade of character or excellence, and *no lower*, than being in agreement and consistent with the structure and connection of the other parts of the organization characterizing the nervous force of each and every individual animal system in which they are severally organized. In the history of physiological lore the anomaly never has presented itself of large, dense, yellow teeth, of the granite-like constitution, ever having been found in the *alabaster* sero-lymphatic temperament, or *vice versa.* Finally, the eruption of the *dens sapientiæ*— wisdom teeth—only tends to increase our puzzled senses. Formed as they are during the full tide of vigorous health and nutrition, in a large majority of persons we find them little better in character and quality than the "milk teeth" of infancy, often making their appearance in the shape of a limy and gelatinous admixture, without organic combination. It is only in those persons of the granite-like, or original strong constituted organization, that we find the *dens sapientiæ* possessing the strong constituents of properly organized teeth.

The elementary constituent difference existing and physically characterizing the deciduous teeth, apart from their size and formation, from the permanent teeth of the adult, is great. The enamel of the milk teeth is nearly of a milk color; it contains less lime and more gelatin than the enamel of the permanent teeth; while the *crusta petrosa* of the necks and fangs, as well as the substance of the teeth, contain more than fifty per cent. of gelatinous matter, so that only with difficulty it can be defined from the bone and its dental periosteum; in short, the milk teeth are constituted little better than enameled ossified cartilage. Here, then, is the proof of the intimate connection of dental pathology with that of the general system; the milk teeth being required only for the temporary purpose of comminuting the softer food suitable to infantile nutrition, they are constructed of more animalized matter, soft, and easily absorbed; and, by the dental organic laws, as the permanent teeth are advanced in their development, the dental absorbents are excited into the action of absorbing the obstructing ridge of the alveoli, as well as the obstructing roots of the temporary deciduous teeth. In vigorous, healthy children this process is gradual and perfect; the fangs are sucked away, until their crowns only remain slightly attached to the gums, when, in a *sound* condition, they are pushed from the mouth.

In the second dentition we find, then, that in agreement, and in accordance with the constitutional peculiarity and strength of development of the individual, gelatin and earthy tissues are in perfect organized union, as the substance of the teeth was originally intended, in its physico-physiological-pathological-mechanical harmony, of construction and organization with the general system of the animal body.

As age advances in accordance with periodic natural changes or cause, the gelatinous tissue is gradually absorbed from the substance of the bone; this may also be observed in the bones of the cranium. The absorption of the gelatinous constituent of the teeth is often prematurely superinduced by the accidents of the *materia medica*, exhibited in diseases of the body, mercury, quinine, iodine, iron, arsenic, etc.; by the smoke and juices of strong tobacco destroying the vitality of the *crusta petrosa;* by continuous indulgence in alcoholic beverages. The slow and continuous absorption of the gelatin tissue leaves the earthy matter in excess, and with this loss of gelatin they are devitalized, until they are left brittle and in a condition of complete atrophy.

It is not my intention to dwell upon the pathology of the first dentition, further than to illustrate the continuity of the constitutional pathognomonic peculiarity of the original foundation of the permanent teeth.

It is well known that the formation of the teeth is begun long before the fœtus leaves the uterus. The process is comparatively slow, and it is not completed until some time after birth. It is not necessary here to trace the original rudiments of the teeth to the third year of their growth,—at which age the child usually possesses all the teeth of the first dentition;—suffice it to say, that these continue in the maxillary bones until the sixth or seventh year, and as the permanent teeth all this time are progressing, we find twenty-eight of these teeth hidden behind the deciduous teeth. The whole process and progress of dental organization to the physiologist, the pathologist, and to the dentist, is as curious as it is instructive.

The general aspect of the first set of teeth in all children is nearly the same, whatever the constitutional peculiarity may be, *although* a very marked difference exists in their elementary constituents. In some constitutions, however, a marked distinction is exhibited even to the most unobservant. It may be seen in puny, weak, strumous, scrofulous, rickety children.

Scrofula and struma are dependent upon a peculiarity of constitution derived from one or both parents. These diatheses are modified by intermarriage. One of the parents being of " good, sound constitution," and the other either strumous, or scrofulous, or phthisical. The children of such parentage present the physical appearances of the diathesis they inherit—a fair and fine skin, light hair, large blue eyes, with dilated pupils, and dull sclerotica, and delicate, transparent complexion. While in others the skin is dark and of peculiar hue, or it is of a rough, dirty appearance; the hair is dark, the upper lip is thick, as if tumefied or swelled; the countenance is sallow or tallowy, and appears swollen, or puffed.

In strumous and rickety children, we are often called upon to prescribe for deficiency of ossific material in the formation and organization of the bones of the osseous system. We find, in these cases, that the natural process of ossification does not progress properly, or that it is at a perfect stand-still; that the bones of the cranium remain in an in-completed condition; that the *fontanelles* and *sutures* do not close; that the teeth not only are slow in their formation, and do not make their eruption until late, but that they are imperfectly constituted, and therefore very imperfectly developed; they are exceedingly soft in texture, and while they are loose in their sockets, the cartilaginous character of the *crusta petrosa* (like that of the milk teeth) is so firmly attached to the lining membrane—periosteum—of the *alveoli*, that portions of the alveolus frequently are brought away apparently conjoined with the bone of the extracted tooth; these teeth frequently exhibiting themselves almost in a state of disintegration; or they are soft, green, painful, loose, and carious. In these persons it will be observed that the os frontis—the bone forming the forehead—is prominent, and the head, though smaller than usual, is generally large in proportion to the face.

In these notes for a memoir on the pathology of the teeth, I do not deem it necessary to describe or to enlarge upon the changes observable in these teeth of scorbutic diathesis; my object having special reference and bearing in illustrating the constitutional marks and characteristics of the several orders and classes of teeth as they are formed and developed in persons differing in constitutional temperaments, and varying in their habits of body or diathesis; whereas, in the third and fourth order of classes, as illustrated by the scorbutic-formed teeth, we find that the animal economy refuses to assimilate nutrition with the requirements of the body—to supply the necessary or normal quantity of elementary constituents for its mathematical or exact organization to represent the highest order of physical development. In these defectively constructed teeth we have a perfect illustration of defective nutrition, or malassimilation of the food with the blood, leading to a deficiency of the phosphates and other constituents required in the organization of hard bones and the ivory-like, hard dental bone. On the other side, again,—for nature is full of opposites, although cause and effect are the same,—we find in the dental organs of scorbutic diathesis *a deficiency* of gelatinous tissue and *an excess of lime,*—too much lime rendering the teeth of calcareous brittleness; whilst the other class presents teeth little else than ossified cartilage; all this, too, in defiance of, and, as it were, in opposition to all our efforts in securing a proper maternal milk; or in the absence of this, "condensed milk," —which is not milk at all,—or cow's, or ass's, or goat's milk, and the several preparations of food which our speculative, experimental knowledge renders us so much more capable of supplying than nature is appropriating. In humility we are compelled to confess that all our efforts appear to be successful no further than the peculiar condition, habit of body, and vital force of the animal system will allow nutrition to be exactly appropriated, or that the illy assimilated metamorphosed blood will supply.

Medical learning, knowledge, and skill, with the practical experience of thousands of years devoted to observing and *curing* the abnormal conditions interfering with nature's intentions, have only added to the accumulation of negative evidence, all of which has been made to culminate in one comprehensive sentence, to wit: " *Improve the general health !"* i.e. *by good nursing!* By good nursing is meant *good food,* of a quality and quantity suitable and adapted to the age and to the digestive powers of the patient: by tonics, by pure air, and all the means *common sense* may indicate. With all these—notwithstanding the well-directed means and appliances of every known chemical and natural remedy, whether in the shape of phosphate, carbonate, change of nurses, and of climate; notwithstanding the child's animal system is at its period of greatest mobility, with the natural dynamics bearing upon the whole animal economy ; while the child has nothing more to do in assisting the metamorphosis of its food, than to eat, drink, play, and rest; yet years often elapse before a change for the better is effected; and even then it would appear that the change is a spontaneous one, produced by the mysterious occult acts of nature, which neither our medical experience, nor our pathological lore, nor the acumen of our observations, can or will furnish us with sufficient cause to explain. Yet we have been gravely told by some writers and some speakers, that at will *they can and do replace the enamel, the substance of the teeth, and even the alveolar processes of the maxillary bones*, by medical treatment and chemical food, even in advanced periods of life. This, too, in the face of the demonstrable truth that after the age of thirty-five atrophy of the fangs may be seen commencing in ninety per cent. of the teeth of the whole human family.

I have thus far indulged in a few practical observations on this interesting, and, to the dentist, highly important subject for his investigation. I offer them with very great deference, hoping that my unpretending "notes" may be accepted as a slight contribution toward a more accurate and sensible dental pathology than has hitherto been permitted to govern the mass of the dental profession, whose panacea for the removal of all dental ills appears to be, either mechanically filling the teeth with foreign substances, or extracting them, and replacing them with artificial substitutes. I am also led into indulging a further hope, viz., that the practical study and careful observations derived from forty years' close application to the medico-surgical practice of the dentist's art, illustrated by these "notes," may prove to be of some value to assist the diagnosis of the dental practitioner, and I add, more especially the *medical practitioner;* for here I may be permitted to observe that I have too often seen instances in the practice of medicine in which the medical attendant and patient were alike placed in an uncomfortable and compromising predicament, in consequence of the want of information, or a contempt for a matter which medical dignity may very erroneously have been in the habit of regarding as being beneath its attention or notice.

Still another hope stimulates and influences me: that the dental practitioner will find and acknowledge that something more remains to be done; that something more is required to make the teeth "endure forever," or even for a lifetime of threescore and ten, than the mere mechanical, expert manipulation of plugging up the hollows in teeth with gold. When we are brought to reflect upon the constant sameness which prevails through the works of Nature, that she constantly moves in a circle, we observe that in the immense variety of developments an inconceivable waste of elementry particles takes place— particles that never reach the parts in the animal organization where they are needed. Does not this apply most emphatically to the dental organs of almost everybody? Look at the enormous quantities of phosphates carried from the system every minute, hour, day, month, and year by the skin and kidney emunctories, by the intestinal evacuations, and by the saliva and other secretions. We were told at the dental convention held in this city two or three years ago, by Dr. White, that he constantly renewed the enamel and the bone of teeth by administering phosphated chemical food. Now, when I tell you that from fifty to one hundred—yes, even to one hundred and fifty—pounds of phosphates, carbonates and other bone material are annually thrown away from the body, perhaps you may be able to arrive at some theoretical conclusion as to what results Dr. White's few grains *per diem* of phosphates might produce in such remote organs as are the teeth. The animal economy avails itself of the nutrition required by the peculiar vital principle acting within and upon each constitution. It appropriates no more and no less than the vital principle stimulating the organs will permit. We will also find that, so long as the constitutions of men differ from each other as they do, so will there be the same great variety in the physical character and pathological condition of their dental organs; that the blood—which is the fluid source from which the teeth, the bones, tendons, muscles, nerves, eyes, hair, membranes, blood-vessels,—in short, every part and atomic particle of the whole organized body—are metamorphosed; that each part is mathematically adapted to its natural, proper place, and yet in so harmonious a manner that the human mind is totally at a loss to comprehend how the arrangements of the operation are performed: but the fact remains. The blood, although comprehensively similar,—I deny that it is exact in man,—yet in each individual it is *sui generis*, or peculiar to himself, and suits and accords with the body *only* to which it belongs and in which it is generated. This peculiarity of blood presents the diathesis or "habit of body" of each particular individual man, woman, and child, and thus with each particular habit of body and temperament the teeth will be found to be in physical and pathological harmony.

For the purpose of illustrating and demonstrating this truth, I have divided the dental organs into four generalized groups or classes, according with their physical appearances, and in connection with, and significant of, the peculiar diathesis and pathological disposition of those constitutions to which I have referred. There are four groups:

I. The large, dense, yellow teeth.

II. The dense, yellowish-white teeth.

III. The chalky-white, the semi-transparent yellow-white, and the dead-yellow, chalky teeth.

IV. The semi-transparent white, the dead, chalk-white, and the bluish-white, pearly teeth.

The possessors of the large, dense, yellow teeth present a solid, firmly-knitted frame, great muscular development, a sound constitution, and full, vigorous health. Those of the second class, while they possess these physical qualities in a less marked degree, their features presenting a softer expression and their lineaments a full and rounded form, do not the less enjoy the general good health allotted to man. The third class, the chalky-white teeth, and the semi-transparent yellow-white teeth, and dead-yellow, chalky teeth, denote a strumous diathesis; and the fourth class, the semi-transparent white, the chalk-white, and the bluish-white, pearly teeth, *so much prized and poetized*, bespeak for the unhappy possessor a predisposition to scrofulous or tubercular phthisis.

To complete these notes upon the pathology of the teeth would require, as you will readily perceive, several evenings to discuss the groups in the order I have presented them to you. I therefore conclude this paper with the remarks, that perhaps there is no region upon the face of the globe that affords such demonstrable proofs of the notes I have presented to you as do the United States; the climate exhibiting the extremes of heat and cold—often varying 40° Fah. between meridian and midnight; moisture is excessive, the rapidity of evaporation extraordinary, and therefore the extremes of humidity and dryness. The effects of such noxious influences upon the general system, thus combined, are too obvious to be lost sight of, nor can these noxious influences be more strongly illustrated than by the impression they make upon the nerves and the development of scrofulous affections. Should the foreigner escape these injurious influences, his offspring suffer to the greatest extent, first among the Irish population, next among the German, and lastly among the Scotch, English, French, Spanish, etc., who, perchance, until this moment, never suspected a taint in their blood; and hence the filling up of the bills of mortality by the thousands with that dire and fatal disorder, "scrofulous consumption."

Thus are they disposed to lament their fate, and ascribe to various causes the rapid decay and loss of the teeth, "when their parents had never lost a tooth." The exemption, however, is only in favor of those retaining, *pari passu*, their original native strength of constitution; and may be accounted for by the order of their lives—the parents partaking regularly of the simplest kind of nourishing food; enjoying, *ex necessitate rei*, plenty of out-door exercise and regular rest, free from mental exaltation, depression, or nervous excitements, and ignorant of such an affection as nervous dyspepsia, or of indigestion, and all their concomitant evils. But here, where the lowliest manage to partake of the most deleterious domestic compounds and luxuries, which in the old countries are either unattainable, or would not be permitted to reach even the tables of the affluent, except upon occasions of friendly hospitality.

Under these circumstances, what can we expect, with our hot-house, modern-improved mode of living, breathing the in-door carbonized and sulphuretted atmosphere, in place of the oxygenated atmosphere, the *one only gift* which God has given to stimulate and purify our blood; never walking when we can ride; never sitting when we can lounge; our only mental excitements, to make money quickly and spend it faster?

In this eagerness after dazzling hoards of Mammon and "brown-stone fronts," in the nervous excitement after ostentatious dissipations, hardly a man or woman, medical or non-medical, ever for a moment pauses to observe the order of nature. Not one of them seems to know, or, knowing, appears to care. In their utter indifference they overlook the fact that each individual is truly, peculiarly, and professedly the pupil of nature; in short, his own physician.

It is the immutable principle of Nature to proceed in every step of her operations by degrees. All outrage and extravagance militate against her established laws. Is it at all strange, then, that the constant abuse and violation of nature's laws should so rapidly fix upon us "all the ills that flesh is heir to," involving "liver complaints," "consumption," scrofulous diseases, etc., and the all-comprehensive dispepsia, with all the horrors of its influence upon the mind and upon every organ of the body? To such an extent does this disorder manifest itself among our people, that indigestion may be considered a national manifestation of gastric debility; the teeth, like the worn-out *vedettes* of a beaten army, giving early tokens of functional or organic disaster.

First Group. The Large, Dense, Yellow Teeth.

In connection with my previous remarks upon the subject of dental pathology, I hope, by this paper, to make clear that, however excellent we may accept art to be, it must be borne in mind that it is generally acquired long before the science is thought of,—and this especially refers to the dentist's art, by accepting which as being infallible, on individual dogmatic authority merely, must tend to retard our advance, endanger our improvement, and, at the same time, to compromise our professional intelligence and honesty; and that the limited authority of true and connected ideas is our only hope of progress and stability, of unity and development.

The science appertaining to the dentist's art is the knowledge of odontology and the pathology of the dental system for the correct treatment and conservation of the teeth. The inquiry, even if with only partial descriptions of the evidences daily presenting themselves to our notice, must serve as a guide in aiding our efforts to elucidate and demonstrate the pathogenic differences in the weaker groups, and the pathological peculiarities exhibited by the perfect organization of the first group of teeth.

We must never forget that we have learned the art of seeing truly; and, fortunately for the progress of the human mind, we live here in an age when every branch of human knowledge is reduced to a popular system; when the most important sciences lay aside the garb of pedantry and mysticism; when, in fine, the access to information is open to all, and the responsibility rests upon us individually, if we do not avail ourselves of the opportunities almost forced upon us.

In our pursuit after knowledge for rendering the comfort of life more effectual and permanent, we cannot help observing that natural philosophy, including chemistry, contributes the principal share in spreading useful information to secure these ends; nor must we omit medicine from this philosophy, for, although considered as a science, it unfortunately rests more upon the practical rules of experience than it does upon mathematical order.

Unfortunately, few persons trouble themselves about a knowledge of Nature; in fact, they remain entire strangers to her ordinary operations, even to cultivating a proper acquaintance with the constitution of their own body, until aroused by the perception of a susceptibility, more or less acute, from some organic lesion or torpor or super-functional derangement, exciting irritability, uneasiness, or pain.

In this respect, perhaps, no other part of the system meets with so much neglect as the teeth,—more especially the teeth of those persons recognized under the general name of "robust constitutions," whose almost iron frame exhibits the hard, dense-constructed bone, covered with full-developed muscular tissue; with great nervous force and vital power; whose respiratory, glandular, gastric, and all the other systems of their body work in unison and harmonious fellowship. It is here, in this well-organized class of human physical perfection, that we find the first group,—the large, dense, yellow teeth; their bone is as hard and as solid as the hardest ivory, and the crystallization of their protecting enamel is as compact as adamant, thus presenting them as the perfection of the dental organization. When we compare these adamantine teeth with the soft, cartilaginous, alabaster-like teeth, —the pearly blue-white of the fourth group,—we find, in the constitutional antitype, the delicate, nervous, hysterical, sero-lymphatic, strumous temperament and diathesis; whose muscular tissue is of soft fibre, and whose blood is deficient in red particles, and who form the large majority of the afflicted called upon to visit the dentist for relief. Now, with this marked difference staring us in the face, I believe that I am safe to say that the dental organs possess their *local*, and, as I will hereafter show, a wide-spread influence in pathological connection with the other parts of the body; and that, in these well-marked extremes, as well as the intermediate conditions of character, the teeth are more or less influenced by the health and condition of the general system; that when the health, strength, and vitality of the body enable it to resist or combat against the destructive onslaught of external and internal agents, the teeth, whatever their constitutional or physical character may be, remain intact; but when the health, strength, and vitality possess neither basis, stamina, or vital force equal to the destructive forces, the dental organs are found at once to yield. Notwithstanding the logic of truth demonstrated by the facts daily presenting themselves to our notice, and notwithstanding that every dentist, almost every day, witnesses the effects of chemical disorganization affecting the teeth in connection with numerous abnormal complications, we are dogmatically told that if these teeth are properly filled with gold "they will last forever,"—if they are filled as *they*, the dogmatists, fill them.

I do not for an instant doubt that the gentlemen insisting upon their own absolute authority, and all its arbitrary assumptions, sincerely believe all they say. But to this I must remark that, if no science exists, then our art ends with the *specific* offered by them, and the various physical character of the teeth is of no consequence. And when we know that not a dentist lives who has *anticipated* and *outlived* his generation; and if it be true, as they have asserted, that none of the older dentists ever filled teeth properly—which I deny—or as perfectly as "*young dentistry*" does, I can challenge them to produce a single case in evidence to prove wherein old people, *retaining* their teeth to the ages of three and fourscore years, have ever had their teeth filled—or, if they have, the teeth have been filled late in life, or they were filled in fissures not "carious."

This cut represents the four groups of teeth.

The teeth and their pathology I shall demonstrate in the classification which I have adopted. They are, severally, affected after their order, as follows: The first group, THE DENSE, YELLOW TEETH, present a firm, solid, permanent appearance, derived from their constitutional healthily supplied and perfectly combined constituents of dental requirements, which, with their complete ossification, and protection by the compact, thick, hard, perfectly crystallized enamel covering the bone, at once exhibits

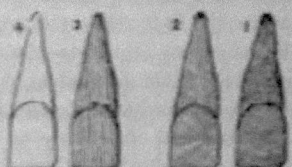

No. 1. First group. The large, dense yellow teeth.

No. 2. Second group. The dense, yellowish-white teeth.

No. 3. Third group. The chalky-white teeth, the transparent yellow-white teeth, and opaque yellow-chalky teeth.

No. 4. Fourth group. The transparent white teeth, the chalky-white teeth, and the bluish-white, pearly teeth.

their character as the best specimens of dental organization.

The teeth of this group rarely decay from any disease of their substance. Their external affections may be traced to functional disorders of the stomach, producing gastric fermentation and the elimination of gastric acids, which find their way along the mucous membrane of the œsophagus, or are eructated into the mouth, mixing with the mucus and saliva, and, as if guided by some peculiar law, fixing upon or selecting certain particular spots or parts of the teeth (for the teeth are affected in the same constitutional or pathological order of decay as eruptive diseases appear in different persons), and, combining with the lime constituents of the selected spots upon the enamel, soften it into what the dentist terms a carious condition of the teeth. In some instances these acids denude the bone of the enamel, leaving the exposed bone with a perfectly even and polished surface, and the teeth remain intact for many years; while in others—the removal of the enamel,—as the tree dies deprived of its protecting bark, so the denuded teeth decay.

Caries in this group of teeth differs from the caries affecting the other three groups. Here we find them in the character of a dark-brown colored, hard, dry, disintegrating rot, which is attended with a styptic, bitterish taste, while we find the process and progress of decay is exceedingly slow. We find the opposite in the third and fourth groups. In these the bone is deprived of its calciferous constituent, leaving a softened, mortified, cartilaginous mass in the teeth; in consistence and appearance it is either like macerated, softened horn, which the operator scoops out in small sheets or flakes, or soaked chamois leather, which is torn from the teeth in solid lumps. This dead, corrupted bone is attended more or less with a fetid taste and a fetid mouth or breath.

In this group of teeth we observe what is never seen in the other three classes of teeth, viz., *the original intention of the dental organization,—the internal vital principle,—*putting forth its powers and exercising its force in resisting the process and preventing the progress of decay; and, while this internal vital force is too feeble to free the healthy from the diseased or dead bone, as is effected in the other diseased bones by the process of exfoliation, its peculiar action is exhibited by a spontaneous cure, produced from the internal dental blood-vessels secreting and depositing in and through the tubuli or pores a new material, *osteo-dentine*, which not only is forced into the capillaries of the dental bone, but also saturates and forms a thick covering over the carious surface, thus furnishing a natural protecting shield.

This secreted and exuded osteo-dentine presents itself a peculiar amber-like, transparent substance, of a yellow-brown color, and, where discoloration of deep brown or black spots are present, they appear like incipient decay, covered with varnish, and polished. Its presence often protects the usefulness of the teeth to the last period of life. When once, however, it begins to decay, it softens, and apparently melts away with great rapidity.

Another source of caries, although of very rare occurrence in this group of teeth, is from accidental defects in the formation of their enamel covering, in the shape of deep fissures in the central depressions, in the enamel upon the grinding surfaces of the bicuspids and molars. The cause of this malperfection may be accounted for in that the process of crystallization is always more perfect when the crystal formations adapt themselves on inclined planes or sloping surfaces; hence the *striæ* of the enamel is seen to radiate directly at right angles from every point of the body of the teeth. In some instances, they do not coalesce, or unite their crystallization in the central depressions on the manducating surfaces of the crowns of the teeth. These depressions may be illustrated by the centre dependent angle in the letter M, which, to a sufficient extent, resembles a section of the bicuspid and molar teeth. The enamel, then, not coalescing in the central part of this depression, forms an imperfect fissure, and offers a receptacle for acrid substances and gastric acids. It is the custom of some dentists to enlarge these fissures through the enamel into the bone, and fill them with gold. However theoretically excellent this practice may appear, my own experience tells me that it is as bad for the teeth as it is for the pockets of their owners, although it proves a profitable practice for those who adopt it. If left alone, they remain free for many years, or, in the course of time, they are obliterated by the wearing down of the teeth, or they are filled in by osteo-dentine.

The next derangement of these teeth occurs at the advancing, and at a late, period of life; and it has puzzled writers not a little to account for this painful affection. My own experience informs me that it is caused by the action of gastric acidified juices, which, although not sufficiently strong to affect the powers and functions of the digestive organs, yet possess sufficient chemical force, when eliminated into and mixed with the mucous and salivary fluids of the mouth, to act upon the surface of the necks of the teeth, frequently, too, implicating the alveolar ridges, causing considerable uneasiness, gradually increasing, as the teeth are more affected, to the most intense sympathetic neuralgia, in the scalp, the neck, shoulders, arms, and even to tingling and pricking sensations in the fingers and toes.* In two cases I have met in practice, neuralgia and spasms of the stomach were the sympathetic symptoms. Another affection of the necks of the teeth consists of deep indented grooves, as if they had been filed into by a three-angled file, or had been worn into by the friction of a hard running cord, the exposed surfaces retaining a highly polished appearance, and entire freedom from sensibility. Then, again, only one or two, or nearly all the teeth, are affected in this manner; the process continues deepening through the necks, until, finally, the crowns of the teeth break off, leaving smooth-surfaced fangs behind; until this separation is effected,

---

* Often treated for nervo-paralytic symptoms.

the bone is so exquisitely tender or sensitive as hardly to permit the touch from a hair. Often, in connection with this abnormal condition, but more generally alone, is the abrasion or wearing away of the enamel of the teeth on their masticating surfaces; this is produced by the chemical action of the gastric and acidified fluids of the mouth, which not only decompose or soften the enamel, but materially assist its mechanical friction while functionally triturating and comminuting the food. And here—only in this group of teeth—is seen the exemplification of the dental vital principle and the internal resources and power that perfectly organized teeth possess for their preservation and the prevention of their loss to the animal economy.

The abrasion of the enamel from the crowns of the teeth is often attended with painful symptoms. The teeth rapidly wearing down, friction and external agents impinge on the nerve-pulps within their chambers, rendering them so exceedingly tender to the touch, that even the softest food causes exquisite sensibility, and partaking of acids, or subacid fruits, or vegetable acid preserves, a thrill of deep-seated pain pervades the jaws, and sympathetically with them the whole system, as if every nerve had received the shock. The same train of painful symptoms is produced by the contact of sugar, sweetmeats, preserved fruits, cakes, molasses, honey, and certain spices, and even by the inhalation or breathing of the atmosphere. Nearly the half of rheumatic and neuralgic affections of the body are the remote symptoms and sympathetic pains of *dento-neuralgia*. In some instances the denuded surfaces of abraded teeth are entirely free from tenderness, and are insensible to the touch; but we often observe one or more concave indented pits in these abraded surfaces, showing dark-red brown stains in the concavities; these stained spots are partially oozed blood, forced, with the osteo-dentine, into the bone from the blood-vessels of the membrane of the internal chambers, which, being in approximation with the external surfaces, causes much distress. The teeth in other instances are worn into serrated points and deep-seated longitudinal grooves upon the cutting edges of the incisors, causing them to form singular meetings of articulation, shutting and interlacing with each other like the irregular cranial sutures, or the aligned teeth of a rat-trap. In others, they wear even with the gums, meeting together as two planes placed in juxtaposition. Another form,—and the only one alluded to by writers, and by them termed *"denudation,"*—is the wasting away of the teeth without any apparent cause, commencing at the central incisors of both upper and lower teeth, and extending on either side to the cuspidati and the bicuspids; so that when the jaws are closed upon each other and the molars meet and touch together, the archings of the superior and inferior front teeth form an elliptical or oblong circle, leaving a space less or more wide between the wasted teeth.

In all these forms of abrasion, or wasting of the teeth, including the grooves in the necks of the teeth, we see the vital principle and ossific resources derived from the internal blood-vessels; and with these resources we observe a very curious natural effort, and its provision, for retaining the teeth to the animal system, viz., that while the nerves, arteries, veins, and membranes are receding, *pari passu*, with the wearing down of the crowns, with this retrogressive process affecting the teeth, the retreating blood-vessels are secreting and precipitating into their unoccupied spaces in the dental chambers, and thence into and through the tubuli, and in continuation forming on the outside surfaces of the denuded bone the same *osteo-dentine shield* which, although not so strong and indestructible as the natural enamel, yet is sufficiently hard and impenetrable to serve and preserve the teeth to an indefinite period of life. And singular it is, that while this vital effort of the internal parts to preserve the teeth is proceeding, the very act destroys the internal vital tissues themselves. The secreted osteo-dentine itself impinges upon the nerves and blood-vessels; and in place of causing inflammatory action, as a gold filling impinging on them would do, they *shrink* away from the gradual oppression until finally they secede from the teeth altogether, but leave the chambers and nerve-canals solidly filled with dentine. This completed, the teeth are insensible to pain. The whole process is perfectly illustrated and demonstrated in the worn teeth of graminivorous animals. Many a noble horse is rendered useless because of the too rapid wearing down of the teeth not allowing sufficient time for the nerves to recede, thereby superinducing acute sensibility or pain that prevents the animal eating sufficient and proper food for nutrition. Swill-fed cows suffer from the same cause and in the same manner.

After the obliteration of the internal vital tissues is completed, the fangs, and such portions of the crowns of the teeth as remain to the animal economy, present entirely different characteristics. They no longer receive nutrition; they are reduced to an inert condition, and all external destructives more or less make their impressions. First we find the dental absorbents sucking away the gelatinous, and then absorbing the lime constituents, leaving only their shrunken, atrophied remains. Here we again often observe another singular process. The absorbents having removed the original bone formation, we find in its place the new-formed, secreted (now) *greenish* amber-like osteo-dentine which had filled the tubuli of the dental bone, and which now, in its diminished character, remains the *substitute*, as it were, of the teeth fangs.

However perfect the organization of the first group of teeth may be, we find them subject to all the vital and destructive forces. They are subject to hypertrophy and atrophy of their fangs. The atrophy is always accompanied by the absorption of the alveolar processes, and the consequent receding of the gums from their necks, by the loss of which the teeth gradually loosen and ultimately fall from the jaws. This annoying affection is known, accepted, and treated by the profession as "*scurvy in the gums!*" In numerous instances the fangs are atrophied at their apices only, which are partially devitalized, and the force of the absorbents is consequently brought to bear upon them,—sucking the apices into sharp, spiculated points, which prick into and irritate the dento-alveolar periosteum, *and also irritating the nerve*, producing sympathetic neuralgic-rheumatic symptoms in various parts of the head, neck, and body. In others, the atrophy causes a thickening, indurated, and partial ossification of the dento-alveolar periosteum, by which the teeth are gradually raised from the bed of their sockets, so that they present various irregular lines of elevation, some projecting far above their fellows. With these elevations the gums recede in the same ratio, when, finally, one after another the teeth drop from their positions —apparently to the inexperienced—in a sound and perfect condition.

Several other pathological conditions exist, but I deem that these I have already mentioned furnish ample proof that the teeth *do* possess a pathology, *and an important one, too;* and I have not mentioned the connection of the great sympathetic nerve with the dento-fifth pair of nerves. With these numerous demonstrative proofs before us,—even including the first-class group of dental perfection,—I challenge any and every dentist in the whole world of our wide-cast profession, by any extra ocular demonstrating proof, to advance a solitary evidence that the mere sheathing or filling in and covering the exposed surfaces of cavities in carious teeth with amalgam, gold, or any other material, however perfectly (mechanically) accomplished, *has ever* or ever will "make the teeth last forever," *i.e.* to the end of old age.

The true knowledge of the pathology of the teeth for the progressive advancement of dental science, extends far beyond the expert manipulation necessary for filling holes in teeth. And once the dignity of its true character being recognized by the light of pathogenic truth, the dental student will appreciate at its proper value all the "Sir Oracle" twaddle of accomplishing odontological impossibilities. By which, too, he will observe a curious pathological anomaly. The fifth pair of nerves is divided into three great branches: first, the ophthalmic; second, the superior; third, the inferior maxillary nerves. The branches, subdivisions, and filaments of the two latter great branches again join and intermix with the ophthalmic branches, and also with the seventh pair of nerves—the nerve of hearing. And, with the common origin and intermixing of the teeth nerves with the ophthalmic nerves, we see an apparent unimpressible, harsh dental pathology connected with that of the exquisitely tender and delicate pathology of the organs of vision.

We must exclaim, How great their extremes, yet how opposite their preservation! Who will not acknowledge the beneficence of the Great Architect of our creation,—that the all-necessary, delicate, wonderful organs of vision should be permitted to escape destruction and disease by only one-half of one per cent. against the ninety-five per cent of the human family losing their teeth? And of the functional disorders of the eyes, five per cent. of them are mere sympathetic impressions produced by dento-nervous irritation. The same phenomenon refers to affections of the ear, and also extends to the scalp, implicating the vast network of nerves spreading throughout the scalp and its tissues, producing pathological changes, by which the force of nutrition is retarded and the roots of the hair are atrophied,—when, like the teeth, the hair becomes thin and ultimately "falls off." The real study of pathology and odontology will explain all these phenomena.

In continuation, I would incidentally remark that the teeth of the first group are firmly fixed in their hard, dense, strong sockets, and that considerable nerve and skill are required to extract them from their articulations without partially breaking them or doing injury to the neighboring parts.

I would also call your attention to the peculiarity of another diagnostic mark in connection with the teeth. I allude to the *salivary calculus*, or tartar, as it is termed,—the calciferous incrustation deposited upon the teeth by the chemical combination of gastric acids with the lime constituents of the saliva. It differs altogether from the tartar deposited on the other classification of teeth. It is exceedingly hard, close, and brittle; of dark, ivy-green color, admitting a high polish. It adheres firmly to the teeth, requiring considerable force to disengage it, which is accomplished with a sharp click sound. It forms a semilunar arch round the enamel outline; sometimes it completely engirdles the necks of the teeth immediately beneath the margin of the gums, rarely extending upon the anterior faces of the teeth.

I conclude these notes upon the pathology of the first group,—the large, dense, yellow teeth; teeth that are only to be seen in the highest order of the physical perfection of man's organization; teeth that are rarely found in a state of malformation or in irregular alignement in their massive, well-developed, well-formed maxillary bones. If we seek throughout the world, and examine the dental conformations of the whole human family, from the highest *caste* of civilization to the lowest grade of savage life, it will be always found that the group of teeth I have described will be possessed by the robust, strong, well-constitutioned, finished, organized specimens of God's exalted creation.

SECOND GROUP.   YELLOWISH-WHITE TEETH.

In my notes on the first group, the large, dense, yellow teeth, I endeavored to lay before the profession the pathology existing between the dental organs and their sympathetic influence upon the whole animal system, wherein I explained the several curious changes occurring in the dental system; and that these abnormal alterations are the proximate causes of the numerous remote dento-neuralgic sympathetic pains produced in the face, ears, head, neck, and various regions of the body.

Before proceeding further with my notes, for the character and dignity of my profession, I deem it pertinent to remark that there are *young* fogies as well as "old fogies," whose minds are equally befogged not only for want of experience and education, but from conceit and ignorance. The object of these notes *is not that of pretension*, but in view of attracting the attention and enlisting the educated talent of the profession, and exciting a more exalted *professional* aspiration than will be content to recline under the ignoble appellation (bestowed upon them by a speaker before the New York Dental Society) of being "tooth-carpenters only;" and to show that it behooves every student of the science pertaining to the dentist's art, to apply his intelligence in searching out and unraveling the pathological phenomena connected with the dental organs and the animal system; and not to accept babbling boasting as a proof of scientific experience—that rotting teeth can be made perfect, and to last forever (which, by the way, periodic family dentists' bills practically contradict); like that ancient boaster and celebrated *insurer of lives*—longevity—Theophrastus Paracelsus, who pretended to possess "the stone of immortality," yet died in his fiftieth year.

No matter—*laudatur ab his, culpatur ab illis*—or, in other words, for us to exercise the faculties with which our Creator has endowed us, whereby the hidden truth may be fathomed, and true knowledge and experience unfolded, by which we may be enabled to adapt a correct treatment; which, if it do not partake of the impossible character, at least may lead to the conservation of the teeth even to good old age. It is much to be regretted, nay, lamented, that we so often see the melancholy exhibition of the *many* whose opportunities are so frequent and brilliant, not only casting aside the proffered gem of observation, but actually closing their eyes, and ignoring their perceptive powers of comparison and description in favor of their *mechanical* view, that *their* mechanical manipulation of the teeth, and *their* mechanical method of filling holes in rotting teeth, with a foreign material, regardless of all pathological conditions, all constitutional diatheses, and all changings of character in the dental organs themselves; yet, like Paracelsus' stone of immortality, they will make the teeth live forever. How truly Shakspeare speaks when he says:

> "In all, designs begun on earth below
> *Fail in the promised largeness;* checks and disorders
> Grow in our veins of action highest reared,
> As knots—by the conflux of meeting sap—
> Infect the sound pine and divert his grain
> Tortive and errant, from his course of growth."

Dullard indeed must he be who does not perceive that the Architect of our nature, when he elaborated our wonderful working animal system, did not place *less* importance upon the physiological intentions of the fifth pair or dental nerves and their numerous branches, than he did upon the second pair, or optic nerves, or the seventh pair, the nerves of hearing.

The professional status of specialists treating the local pathological affections of "the eye and ear," in connection with constitutional medical and surgical treatment, is acknowledged by the medical faculty, wherever the science of medicine and the surgeon's art are practiced. The highest order of medical erudition and practical experience is demanded of the oculist and aurist to enable him to treat these organs successfully. With these credentials they are recognized by the medical profession, and accepted by the community, as important auxiliary branches to surgery and to the healing art.

May I ask why, or how, it is that the educated dentist does not command the same professional appreciation and respect of the medical faculty and the community at large? The answer is readily made. Because the majority of the dental profession are content to impress upon them the *mechanical exaltation* which they receive from their personal patrons!—as the *alpha* and *omega* of surgico-dental excellence; that the condensation of dento-professional accomplishments exists solely in their individual method of filling carious teeth with gold or amalgam, the uniqueness of which method will make them last forever. Surgeons, physicians, oculists, aurists,—and even dermatologists,—nor chiropodists, nor advertising quacks,—do not thus commit themselves. Thus by dentists themselves the public is educated to think,—urged into the belief, and *impressed with the one idea*—that the dentist's art extends no further than mechanically filling holes in decayed teeth, extracting and making artificial "dentures" substitutes. Mechanical art requires no learning; it requires no erudition; while it brings ready money. But erudition, professional learning, and professional status are boasted of, as adjuncts, as an artist is compelled to place his picture in a gilded frame; *but they do not pay* like mechanical dentistry! Besides, education costs *time, brains,* and *money;* therefore the mechanical dentist ignores professional learning as unnecessary, and pins the faith of the public not upon his professional acquirements, but upon his mechanical tooth fillings as he fills them. With singular contradiction, the same public does not hesitate to be physicked for their eyes and ears by the oculist and aurist; and poison their hair with destructive dyes and "bleachings," and paralyze and destroy their eyes with *belladonna;* and be fleeced by the dermatologist, and even to be patented into their graves by vile quack medicines; yet this same public will not take a prescription from a dentist unless it be a fifty-cent bottle of "detergent tooth-wash," or a box of tooth-powder. That I do but speak the truth, read how I am sustained by the statement of G. C. Daboll, M.D., published in a Western journal:

"At no time," says this gentleman, "in the history of dental science, has the profession made such sure and rapid progress as since the inauguration of dental societies. This progress cannot be attributed to 'dental schools,' for *not one* dentist in a hundred ever attended one. In the clinical department the dental association takes the character in a measure of a dental college; it has been the only school for many a good operator of to-day." There is a dentist in this city that never went to school at all. He says that dental colleges and dental associations are humbugs. Teeth must be filled as he fills them, and they will last forever.

The city of Baltimore and the city of Philadelphia have the honor of having inaugurated dental schools, and to the zeal and accomplishments of their several professors the dignity of the profession is indebted for the name of "American Dentist" being respected in every part of the world where he may make his appearance. To these collegiate dental schools the United States are eminently indebted for the general advancement of dental professional learning, experience, and improvements in the science of the dentist's art. From dental schools have been distributed the *pabulum* which has fed and is feeding Dr. Daboll's "hundred" that never attended school. Numerous railroads lead and point their tracks to the portals of the Baltimore and Philadelphia dental schools, where dental professional instruction is open to them. The sooner they matriculate the better for themselves, and certainly the best for benefiting the teeth, and their sympathies of an enlightened public; and the sooner scholastic dental education is rendered a necessity, the sooner the professional dentist will be acknowledged to be an equal professional with the oculist and aurist.

The efforts of our dental schools must teach the public mind that the art of the dentist is something more than mechanical. It is a serious misfortune to medical science, as it is an opprobrium upon the dental profession, that so little, if any, attention is devoted to acquire an acquaintance with, and a knowledge of, the symptomatology of dental pathology. The physician is content to leave the apparently to him insignificant, undignified, rotting teeth to the *mechanical treatment* of the dentist, entirely ignorant of the many severe, remote sympathetic symptoms which he, when "called in," treats as idiopathic derangements of the regions of the body complained of by the patient. The dentist is content to treat carious teeth, as mechanical organs, mechanically; he, with the physician, being equally innocent of their remote sympathetic and symptomatic affections.

The second group, the yellowish-white teeth, in the order of dental pathology, are possessed by that class of people of cholerico-sanguine and phlegmatic-sanguine temperaments. These teeth contain more gelatinous tissue or constituent, consequently they are whiter in color and less dense in their bone and enamel structure; hence they are more delicate in their nature, compared with the first group; and although not so solid, they still present a firm, strong appearance, while their size and lineaments display a softer and more pleasing expression to the "human face divine." It is with difficulty that the first class of teeth can be cut, filed, or drilled into, with the finest-tempered steel instruments. These teeth, on the contrary, although constituted with a high degree of hardness, more readily yield to the mechanical appliance of dental instruments. They are more easily acted upon by the gastric acids. They decay more rapidly, the mortified part being moist, sometimes soft, of a dirty light-brown color, while the decay in the first group is a yellow-brown color, dry, disintegrating rot, rough and stringent to the tongue, and resembling the *débris* of the tan-pit. The softer enamel and bone of the second class, of course, can be cut, drilled, filed, and carved into, with more ease and with greater facility.

The *dens sapientiæ*—wisdom teeth—unlike those of the first group, which invariably exhibit a perfect condition, often make their appearance defective in their organization; the defect is confined to the central depression in the masticating surface. These imperfections speedily run into decay, producing neuralgic symptoms of less or greater intensity either in the cuspidati, bicuspids, or in the anterior molar teeth, where the bicuspids are absent. The symptoms are various, from a simple headache to uneasy sensations of a tingling, creeping nature; a sensation of tightness, or pulling, or diffused soreness over the scalp; acute paroxysms of lancinating, shooting pains in the right or left temporal region, in the right or left ear, or a dull aching to acute neuralgic distress at the back of the head, and down the nape of the neck. In severer symptoms, the paroxysms extend to the supra-orbital nerve, above the eye and extending to the forehead; to the sub-orbital nerve, under the orbit of the eye, to the cheek-bone, extending to the face— the "*tic douloureux*" of the French—and sometimes to the nose, causing chronic catarrh of this organ; spasmodic stricture of the gullet—pseudo-gastralgia; in the right or left eyeball attended with motes, webs, and congeries of snake-like formations of various sized rings, small, black or transparent disks, with occasional brilliant scintillations of nervo-electric light, vulgarly known as "seeing stars." These dento-neuralgic, sympathetic symptoms are invariably treated as *amaurotic* affections. Then an acute concentred pain on the apex or "crown" of the head; prickling and tingling or creeping sensation in the arm, forearm, hands, or fingers, which are treated as paralytic symptoms. In many cases, however, the sympathetic pain of diseased wisdom teeth is confined to the anterior bicuspid tooth, and, where it is absent, to the anterior molar tooth. These are the sympathetic pains which for illustration I limit to the head, neck, and arms only. A remarkable diagnostic characteristic denoting the exciting cause specially referring to the above-named regions, is that *the sympathetic pain is always on the same side as the affected tooth*, and, as a rule, *never passes over the mesial line of the head and face to the opposite side.* It must be borne in mind that no pain is experienced in the wisdom tooth itself during these paroxysms, or at any other time of intervals.

The illustration represents the central incisors of a young lady, 4th class teeth, treated for five years medically for ozæna, catarrhal neuralgia, and neuralgia of the supra-orbital nerves. Fig. 1, right incisor:

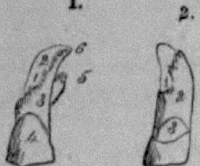

2, the original form of the root; 1, the serrated edge; 3, the remaining portion of the fang; 4, body of the tooth, lateral decay; 5, bone node-exostosis; 6, apex absorbed. Fig. 2, left incisor partially absorbed: 1, hollow into which the node of fig. 1 fitted; 2, remaining serrated fang; 3, decay in the anterior face and neck of the tooth.

The teeth are sometimes in sympathetic affection with constitutional irritability, or nervous depression; in either case relapsing fever is the attendant, so mild in its character as to be simply characterized "feverishness" or "cold;" but sufficient, however, to affect the action of the heart, and implicate the mucous membrane of the *primæ viæ* and skin, with general muscular debility—perhaps better understood by the popular description, "running down of the system." The mucous membrane of the mouth presents the index, which, with the gums is swollen by sub-effusion partaking of the emphysematous character; they are of a deep red, or pale color; the gums are flaccid and covered with a viscid mucus, and hang loose against the teeth. The teeth are partially loosened from their positions by the thickening of the alveoli periosteum within the sockets. Sometimes a watery exudation of acid character eats into the necks of the teeth; at other times an acid pus is suppurated from the edge of the gums, which is the cause of much local distress; while the functions of mastication render them very painful. The teeth spread apart from each other, and in connection with the gums are exquisitely sensitive, whether by the presence of sweetmeats, acids, surgico-dental instruments, teeth-brush, and even drawing the breath upon them. A soft, viscous, mixed salivary calculus is largely deposited upon them.

The same indented formation is observed in this as in the first group, but with more natural fissures in the enamel of the masticating surface, which too often meet with the same infamous usage as those in the first group, by having auger-holes bored into their substance, and the removed healthy enamel and bone replaced with a foreign material, proposed as a *mechanical* prophylactic against the action of *chemical* agents and future decay.

Exostosis, or dental *nodes*, show themselves particularly upon this group. Exostosis differs in a measure from the hypertrophied conditions of the teeth, inasmuch as the latter exhibits almost a uniform swelling of the enlarged bone; the nodes present hard, circumscribed, round or oblong, knotty tumors, formed near to or upon the apices of the fangs. An interesting specimen, unique of its kind, I recently exhibited before the New York Dental Society. It was, as it were, the anchylosis of the inferior wisdom tooth and the two adjoining molar teeth. They were united by solid, continuous, conglomerated, nodular bone excrescences, presenting a formation as if the teeth had taken root in a young bone-reef. The wisdom tooth and posterior molar tooth, years before their extraction, had been filled with gold, which still remained as perfect as when first introduced into the teeth.

Under certain constitutional aberrations occurring in the system, the mucous membrane of the *primæ viæ* secretes a peculiar acid, by the chemical action of which upon the metals placed in the hollows made, or in the carious cavities formed in the substance of the teeth, an electro-galvanic impression is produced upon the dental bone, nerves, blood-vessels, and periosteum, at each and every period when the mucous membrane is brought into the condition to produce and secrete this acidified mucus. The process, therefore, is intermittent and slow, consequent upon the intervening periods of health, alternating with the periods of functional or organic disquiet. From this incertitude of action, years often elapse before the effects are recognized. For very many years this electro-galvanic action of metals has been recognized by dentists in connection with artificial teeth set on metallic bases. The mischief often done to the remaining sound teeth is patent to every dentist. But they have never taken the trouble to investigate the matter, and certainly they have never devoted a thought to the electro-galvanic action of metal fillings in carious teeth. And here again we observe how nature deals out her opposites, although excited from the same cause. First, the electro-galvanic action produces a super-excitation of the dental absorbents, which suck away portions of the apices of the fangs, leaving sharp, needle-like spiculated points, which are the immediate cause of various irritations,—alveolar periostitis, abscess, tumefactions, and pains in the jaws, etc. The second electro-galvanic super-excitation stimulates the dental nerves and blood-vessels into an extra nutritive effort, and exostosis of nodular bone formation upon the roots of the teeth is the result. Sometimes we observe both the absorbent and nutritive forces acting together upon the dental roots; on one side the absorbents suck away the substance, while on the other side exostosis is forming nodes of bone, as if nature would replace that which she is taking away. These enlargements upon the fangs of the teeth cause corresponding absorption of the alveoli sockets, to make space for these protuberances extending from the fangs, which not unfrequently cause a thickened and permanent induration of the alveolar periosteum; oftentimes forming painful tumors, but most frequently chronic ("gumboils") fistulous openings, which heal and ("break") suppurate at various indefinite periods. (See *Figs*. 1 and 2, page 28.)

And thus when the innocence of mechanical art engages in a contest with nature's perfection of healthful organization, no rhetoric of the pen, nor the logic of reason, is required to explain the results of mechanically applied causes of irritation. There is but one state of health. It is more mathematically sensitive to changes than even the best equalized balance; and if anything is forced against the equipoise of perfect, healthy organs, whether against the stomach or the teeth, etc., nature resents the outrage made against her immutable laws by producing deviations not in favor of the disquieted organs; and thus we find that exostosis forced upon healthy teeth whose fissures had been unnecessarily tampered with.

As with the first group, the gums and dental periosteum are subject to acute, subacute, and chronic inflammation. In the majority of cases the chronic affection is passive loss of tone. In the first form the dento-maxillary periosteum descends into the suppurative condition, receding from the fangs and from the alveolar ridge, beginning at the molar teeth on one side, and traveling round the jaw to the corresponding teeth on the opposite side; occasionally implicating the periosteum of the whole maxillary bone. The periosteum then recedes from the fangs of the teeth, and leaves the alveoli denuded; the teeth stand loosely attached in their now diseased periosteal bed, and ultimately fall from the jaws in an apparently sound condition; but, upon examination, the fangs present a semi-transparent appearance produced from causes already mentioned, and the maxillary bone will be found partially honeycombed from the action of the absorbents. This is sometimes diagnosed for malignant disease.

Irregularities or mal-alignement of the teeth here assume a more marked derangement. It is the generally accepted opinion that deficiency of space or contraction in the maxillary bones is the reason why the teeth cannot be admitted into their uniform positions in the maxillary circle. A remarkable natural consistency presents itself in the conformation of infant jaw-bones and teeth. Never, unless in deformed, rickety children, or in cases of *mollities ossium*, so far as my extended experience serves me, do we meet with malformed jaws or dental irregularities in the first dentition; and it is rare, indeed, that we ever find any deviation; as far as regards the circular space, necessary to the symmetrical arrangement of the teeth in their maxillæ. But we do find deviating malformations and malconformations in the maxillary bones and the alveolar processes in adults—that is, in the second dentition—which cause the various "irregularities" I speak of.

It would appear that the alveolar processes are mere auxiliary ridges of bone sockets, intended for the time only that the teeth remain in their positions; that upon the removal of the teeth from their sockets, whether by disease, accident, or surgically, the absorbents are immediately brought into action, and do not cease until they are entirely removed; and by an opposite action again the periosteum secretes a smooth bone covering in the place of the absorbed alveolar processes, so that the non-anatomist, ignorant of pathological and physiological compensations, would never suspect that teeth had crowned the smooth, rounded surface of the maxillary bone.

Dental associations and authors have always dwelt with particular emphasis upon contractions of formation of the maxillary bones, as being the cause of the deviating and crowding irregularities of the teeth from their natural symmetrical positions. Contradicting this singular anatomical error or oversight, upon even superficial examination, it will be seen by ocular demonstration that the maxillary bones— *upon which the alveolar processes or sockets are formed and placed*— are always of proper proportions, and of ample dimensions for the perfect arrangement of the teeth.

Analytic chemists furnish us with elaborated analyses of the bone, the enamel, and the crusta petrosa of the teeth,—as they do of the blood,—but no two chemists agree as to the mathematical composition of each part. Their figures and quantities all vary. The reason is obvious. Examine the character of the four groups of teeth I have named by separate chemical analysis, and each group and each subdivision will demonstrate different analysis of constituent atoms. The alveoli partake of these differences. All this time we are constantly reminded by unpractical theorists of the atomizing, cellular, and molecular germinations, arrangements, and combinations of nutrition that are called upon to make the rudiments into the ultimate formation of the teeth. Vigorous, healthy, natural formations assume, in their order, their intended natural proportions and symmetry. Weak or delicately

constituted teeth and alveoli deviate from the intended normal proportions both as regards size and outline. These influences produce their
effects, first, upon the physical character and outlines of the jaw-bones,
—which are always ample,—and then upon the alveolar processes,
which are either protruded forward or contracted inward of their circles
at angles of abnormal inclinations; the latter producing an aberrating
space that will not permit them to contain the now overcrowding teeth
in their order of symmetrical alignement. Thus, with a very little
observation bestowed upon this phenomenon of construction, the peculiar dynamics affecting them will demonstrate the character of each
irregularity of the alveoli, and the consequent derangements of the
teeth.

To render my remarks more clear. The examination of the infant
skeleton maxillary bones, displaying the progressing second dental
forming organs behind the first dentition complete, will illustrate an
apparent intermixing of bundled portions of half made-up teeth. How
they are conveyed to their distant positions, alignements, and meet
together in their beautiful conformations of articulation, I must leave
to the erudition and philosophy of Dr. Daboll's hundred scientific dental
experts, who have never been to a dental school, to explain. They will
do it!

The conformation of the upper jaw-bones makes the foundation of the
face. Unlike those of the lower jaw, the alveolar processes spread or
diverge in conical shape from the palato-maxillary bones at an angle
similar to the inverted letter $\bigwedge$. To conform with this outstretching,
radiating formation of the alveolar processes and teeth of the upper
jaw,—while we observe the anatomical *necessity* of the lower jaw being
all spacious and capacious to form a recess for, and to allow the free
action of, the tongue and muscles within their osseous circumvallation,
—we also observe that the outward circular dimension of the jaw too is
great, if the teeth were articulated *upon* the maxillary bone proper, to
meet even the outstretching, antagonistic teeth of the upper jaw. We,
therefore, find that the alveolar processes of the lower jaw are formed
with an *inward* inclination, which, with the prolonged inclination of
the teeth, shows by a plumb-rule from the inner edge-line of the corona
of the molar teeth that their masticating surface line is inside of the
maxillary ridge proper from one-third to three-quarters of an inch.

The deficiency of space, then, caused by the increased inward inclination—less or more—of the dental processes, clearly explains the cause
of the physical deformities, while it mathematically illustrates the dis-
arrangements of the teeth. The lower jaw of the first group of teeth,
in many instances, presents the "bold, *square* jaw," in which the
central incisors and the two cuspidati partially lap the two lateral
incisors, in consequence of the squaring of the alveolar circle in

of the animal creation, however, possess the great advantage over exalted reasoning humanity,—a perfect-working, healthy stomach,—which produces healthy and uncontaminated fluids, and, as Shakspeare has it, "sweet breath."

A sound stomach is absolutely necessary to a sound body, and a sound body is as equally necessary to a sound mind; and as the enjoyment of a sound mind in a sound body is the greatest of all terrestrial blessings, it is incumbent on every rational inquirer to devote a portion of his time to the research of such useful objects as may contribute to improve, and, if possible, to insure a state so desirable. In an eminent degree, then, may weak, suffering humanity look to dental science not only as a benefactor, but for relief from a very distressing portion of "the ills that flesh is heir to."

The ancients conceived the idea of " *a principle of life*," which they compared to " *a radical fluid!*" The alchemists expected to find this *original entity in gold*, by the use of which they pretended that the human body might acquire the solidity and durability of that metal. EUREKA! Some dentists, at this late day of scientific knowledge and insight into natural philosophy, apply the same pretensions to natural rotting teeth; that by the application of amalgam, or gold,—as they apply it,—the original entity of the teeth is to be rendered as durable, as dense, and as solid as they pack these materials into the teeth.

With the third group of teeth—apart from the pathological conditions of the previous groups—the perplexities, the obstacles, the difficulties, and the vexatious humiliations of the dentist really begin. In the previous groups an innate constitutional vigor assists the dentist, and renders his endeavors permanent for a reasonable time of wear and tear, as well as against numerous destructive causes. But here, with these teeth, he has to contend with and against almost insurmountable constitutional, natural, physical, and *moral* obstacles. First, constitutional debility of the habit of body; second, external and internal agents working their destruction; third, the physical imperfection of the organization of the teeth themselves; and last,—and far from being the least,—the dental surgeon! not being allowed the medical privilege of applying a constitutional treatment to improve the general health, even where the susceptibility of impression is intensified by chronic anæmia, nervous debility, or any other cachectic diathesis; the influences of which, upon the dental organs, increase the destructive process faster than dento-mechanical ingenuity—in lieu of proper medical treatment—can resist them. That he is denied this common-sense view and privilege of constitutionally treating with the view to reclaim *a debilitated dental organization*, the conservation of which he has selected as his "specialty," the dental practitioner has none others "to thank," and only *himself* to blame for the negative medico-dento-surgical position he holds in the

overcome fretfulness, "nervousness," caprice, restlessness, and *inatten-tion* which, with really high, nervous, hysterical temperaments, bodily debilities, bad breath, *fear*, and other pathological antagonisms of the patients, are part of the exhausting embarrassments which combat the dentist's most zealous efforts.

Notwithstanding the fearful experience of wear and tear upon the operator's nerves, by all, we listen monthly to artisans and apothecaries who, as a *dernier ressort*, pick up the profession *as a trade*, and who, by their own conceited approbation, elect themselves the oracles of dental in-fallibility, and before their dental associations, and at their "odontologi-cal meetings," exalt *their* "method" of making the dental organs last forever, by comprehensively sopping creasote into teeth daily, for months, and then "leaving a little sop of the creasote in the fangs and filling over it;" forgetting—that is, assuming that they ever were aware of the circumstance—that the dental system, apart from chemical and other destructive causes, and mechanical wear and tear, is equally liable and exposed to be affected from constitutional derangements, acid, gout, rheumatic, and mercurial secondary diathesis, febrile derangements, gas-tric irritations of the mucous membrane of the digestive organs, stoma-titis, dyspepsia, indigestion, cutaneous diseases, etc., which can be only reached by that treatment which strikes at the root of the remote and ex-citing cause ; or by means of improving the general health, and thereby stimulating and assisting the *vis medicatrix naturæ*, or in other words giving increased force to the vital healing powers of Nature, that by her beneficent laws the exciting cause may be destroyed.

I most earnestly desire that my remarks may not be construed as re-flecting, *in the remotest manner*, upon educated gentlemen whose pro-fessional endowments are not only distinguished, but who, I proudly acknowledge, daily add new lustre to the importance of the dental art, and who would, doubtless, be gratified to have the public and the medical faculty draw a line of demarkation, by placing the educated of the pro-fession upon the exalted footing which its true character demands, as being an auxiliary part of—as it is admitted into the most distinguished London hospitals—and collateral science with the healing art. My hints refer to the pathological moral of the dental profession *at large*, showing that respectable, true knowledge is equally important in its connection with these hints upon the true pathology of the teeth and their scientific, conservative treatment.

I have subdivided the third group into three classes, the organi-zation of which is represented by their physical character, and which presents them in their highest original physical grade of appearance, to their descending modifications, which might be extended under the head of subdivisions ; some presenting a chaotic ossification of accretions, covered with a semi-crystallized mottled-colored enamel; others exhibiting a smooth enamel of a dark cloudy hue, with dirty-looking lime-spots surrounded by dirty-appearing yellow margins, or dirty-yellow lime-spots slightly raised and surrounded by dirty-white margins. Others again present a chaotic combination of cartilage, bone, lime, and enamel admixture. These several orders of teeth exhibit the true and peculiar characteristic diathesis of each and every individual or family constitutional organization. And if blood will tell in no other instance can functional discrepancies of the secretory processes be more clearly observed and defined as furnishing and forming imperfectly organized material and exhibiting hereditary tendencies and constitutional predispositions than in these teeth. The only digression may be attributed to a curious but well-established phenomenon—that is the disappearance or omission of constitutional tendencies during one generation to appear in the next. This has been termed Atavism.

It is not uncommon in addition to the teeth being inherited from one or the other of parents or ancestors to observe them blending the constitutional character of both. For example, the front teeth exhibiting the superior organization of the one parent and the back molar teeth presenting the strumous or phthisical etc. of the other, and vice versa.

Lime predominates in this class of teeth—hence their structure is soft and brittle. They frequently "crumble away" in the mouth without apparent cause; but which is explained by certain conditions—and they are more certain than otherwise—of the system. These conditions are too often superinduced by mode of living, want of pure air, the need of out-door exercise, lack of nutrition, i.e. non-assimilation of the food with the blood, overstudy, overwork, overheated sleeping apartments, mental anxiety, pneumo-gastro-enteric debility, respiratory hysteric nervous affections etc.; the result of which is nervous dyspepsia and all its concomitant evils, not the least of which is the elimination of sulphur, etc. and other equally obnoxious gases—hence foul breath, wind and puffed stomach, the generating and elimination of phosphoric lactic carbonic and other acids, all of which produce their several deleterious influences.

In the sublimity of the perfection of the Creator's work the evidence of organization demonstrates that the teeth should not be encumbered with peculiar and inevitable elements of early decay. Nature cannot resist the same etc. Doubtless Nature's design is to render her organization as firm and as solid as the oak, and that the teeth shall be of sufficient enduring strength with power of resistance to last until age atrophies them; that their permanence shall be no longer required than to be useful to the body, and then—as in the lower order of animals—to fall from the mouth. As Shakespeare describes decadence:

" Last scene of all,
That ends this strange, eventful history,
Is second childishness, and mere oblivion,
Sans teeth, sans eyes, sans taste, sans everything."

To preserve the teeth to this end, how grandly beautiful and simple is Nature's provision and arrangements for the protection of her remotest equally important organs! Natural animal chemistry in her silent laboratory of the animal economy, through the functions of the salivary glands, elaborates an *antiseptic alkaline* fluid,—the saliva. While the stomach remains in its healthy and normal functional condition, no more acids are generated than are necessary to the chemical process of digestion; but when the acids, by any accident, are in excess, the alkaline saliva directly neutralizes them; and when these acid eliminations exceed the neutralizing power of saliva swallowed, "acid stomach," acid eructations, "water-brash," "heart-burn," etc. are the results. These acids, either eructated or "worked" up the mucous membrane into the mouth, meet the saliva freshly poured from the salivary glands. A chemical combination takes place,—with whatever acid it may be,—and the phosphated, oxalated, or carbonated lime, etc. is precipitated and deposited upon the teeth, mixed with various matter of the mouth, throat, and lungs, and forming (in these constitutions) the filthy, pasty substance, termed "*tartar*," sometimes in disgusting quantities. Singular as it may appear,—as a rule,—this filthy accumulation protects the parts of the teeth it covers, from the onslaughts of the super-excess of acids. As the mechanical action of coughing is produced by an irritation physiologically intended to relieve the respiratory organs of offending matter, the very act of coughing, by its reflex action, super-excites and increases the irritation, and the consequent exhaustion of the nerves of respiration, that its functions are intended to relieve. In like manner the chemical combination depositing the tartar, while it protects the teeth one way, seriously injures them in another way, by mechanically pressing the gums from the necks of the teeth,—their most delicate and tender part,—or by causing inflammation of the gums and their suppuration, and by gradually insinuating itself between the teeth and gums, and impinging upon the bone sockets, causing them to recede by exciting the absorbents to act upon them, and the loosening of the teeth consequent upon the loss of their osseous support. *Obsta initus*—check the beginning of evil by removing it.

It is worthy of remark, that salivary calculus is never deposited adherent to the sockets of the teeth, and although pounds after pounds of phosphate and carbonate of lime are chemically formed and precipitated from the vital fluids of the animal economy,—sufficient in quantity, after a year or two, to furnish material to *reconstruct* a hundred sets of second or even third dentition, but all of which is swallowed into the digestive laboratory, or expectorated from the mouth, and is forever lost to the animal economy,—yet, with this singular proof staring us in the face, we are told, in all seriousness, by some, that they daily recuperate, reconstruct, and re-establish anæmic and cachectic teeth, and renew their bone sockets with as much certainty as the genial rays of the vernal sun prepare the atrophied grass for the vigor of its summer luxuriance. All this is effected, too, by a few grains of scientifically prepared manure, in the shape of phosphated medicaments.

Constitutional aberrations frequently cause the salivary glands and mucous membranes of the mouth, etc. to secrete *acidified* in place of the alkaline fluid. With this acid diathesis the teeth decompose very rapidly; the enamel presenting the appearance of a dirty-yellow, a dirty-white, or a white-bleached calcined chalky substance, as if burnt by the agency of fire. This acid-affected enamel and softened bone dentists term "white decay." The corrupted bone is exquisitely sensitive, and difficult to be explained, for when removed the healthy bone beneath—in a large number of cases—is insensible to the touch of the instrument. What an everlasting blessing to suffering humanity, and what a chance for infallible dental oracles to prove their assertions by demonstrating before Dr. Daboll's never-went-to-school dental clinics *their* method of making these teeth last forever!

The teeth, we know, are alkaline; and we also know that acids soften and decompose their substance. Some acids, however, have less affinity for lime than others; these penetrate the pores of the enamel, and, while they do not actually combine with the lime chemically, they destroy the vitality of cohesion. Soda (Vichy) water, bread, cakes, tea-biscuit, etc., containing an excess of saleratus, this alkaline combines with the acid contained in the pores of the bone and enamel, and by the sudden evolving of the gas produced by the chemical union of acid and alkali, produces a diminutive miniature process of "blasting," causing a disintegrating or "crumbling away" of the teeth. This circumstance has furnished an idea to those who jump at conclusions, that saleratus is a destructive agent to the teeth. Some years ago, in the solemn council of a dental convention, the meeting recorded its opinion "that the saleratus we use in the manufacture of our bread is the cause of the early destruction of the teeth,"—Dr Baker indorsing the debate with the statement that *he* "found that in a solution of saleratus a set of teeth was destroyed in two weeks." Yet, again we see opposites producing the same effects. After long debility,—whether the concomitant of anæmia, gestation, lactation, or *obscure* causes,—and health again restored, the salivary glands secrete a healthy alkaline saliva, and the stomach is free from abnormal gastric acidity. We find that with the debility of the system the teeth have been sympathetically—(as, indeed, all teeth are in all constitutional debilities)—affected. "Oh, doctor, I have been ill a long time and my teeth are all gone to ruin," is the exclamation in every dentist's practice. Thus debilitated, the teeth to a certain extent are made more porous and less vital; they are saturated with the alkaline saliva—(one of the physiological, anti-septic, alkaline purposes of this fluid is intended to protect the teeth)— and the contact of acids, whether from vinegar-pickles, vinegar-salads, lemons, etc., produces the same chemical evolutions and the same "crum-bling away" or gradual disintegration.

The transparent-yellow teeth with blue edges present the first order of teeth organized with an excess of gelatinous tissue. Their texture and structure, as a consequence, render them soft. In the first class of this group the operator oftentimes, when cutting down through the decayed portion of the tooth, slips the instrument into a lime accretion of bone, causing acute pain. This is often mistaken for nerve-tissue, and mischief is frequently done by the application of arsenic and other corrosive poisons for the purpose of destroying the nerves. These cor-roding, irritating agents, under such circumstances, do not reach the nerve-tissue, but they poison the substance and vitality of the gelatinous bone. A second and a third time arsenic is inserted into the teeth, and acute inflammation of the nerve and periosteum is superexcited, and, there being no outlet for the decomposed nerve-matter, which, like de-composed brain-matter, is exceedingly poisonous, INTRO-DENTAL ABSCESS is formed, with all its grievous concomitant evils, even to caries, necrosis, and exfoliation of the jaw-bone itself. Sometimes the dental instru-ment encounters an almost cartilaginous substratum, the opposite of the lime accretion; the pain, if possible, is more acute. The color of these teeth, under ordinary circumstances of the death of their sub-stance, is altered to a dark-greenish purple or blue-green hue; and in none, the succeeding group excepted, have the structure and substance of the teeth so high a degree of sensibility as has this cartilaginous bone organization. This "*sensitive dentine*," by which it is known in dental nomenclature, can be recognized as proving Dr. Horner's *materia vitæ diffusa* and Hunter's nervous matter in the vital fluids.

The necks of these teeth are acutely delicate—(as indeed the necks of all teeth are their most tender part)—and sensitive to external agents; and notwithstanding the subject of the *mischief done to the necks of the teeth* by "ill-adapted dentures"—(meaning the clasps by which artificial teeth are secured to the natural teeth)—is an annual dish served up before dental associations to argue upon, they recommend the use of floss silk—with its acute fibres—to be drawn between the teeth to cleanse, rather say, cut into them. And one doctor (a New York dentist?) offers "for sale at the dental depots and principal drug-gists in New York and Philadelphia" what he euphoniously and deli-cately terms THE LADY'S (!) TOOTH PRESERVER. In the fullness

of his simplicity he asks for information—" Why do the teeth decay
' *between*' them ?" He enlightens himself by answering his own philosophical question: " Because food remains in the spaces long enough
to undergo fermentation, which produces an acid that acts upon the
enamel and eats it away." The doctor then recommends "the fillet
of rubber to pass readily where no toothpick will go; and *naively*
adds: " It"—the fillet of rubber; the Lady's Tooth Preserver—"will
also indicate by a slight feeling of tenderness *when* the teeth require
the services of a dentist." And this is dental science! The merest
tyro, studying physiological intention, ought to know, *that upon the
healthy, compact, firm embrace of the gums to the necks of the teeth
mainly depends their solidity in their sockets, their permanence,* and
usefulness free from uneasiness. Common sense indicates this truth.
By this unpardonable ignorance the gums are not alone irritated, but
the necks of the teeth also, and the crusta petrosa is ultimately destroyed; by the destruction of which the gums never adhere to the
necks of the teeth again. The gums are rendered " spongy," " flabby,"
etc.; they are tender and bleed upon the slightest touch ;—a tendency
they possess in these constitutional diatheses without the addition of
ignorant, outrageous, superexciting causes.

In addition to the injury perpetrated upon the necks of the teeth by
destroying the adhesion of their protecting, warming, nourishing gums,
external irritating agents excite the dental absorbents into activity,
which suck the vital parts from the roots, producing atrophy, looseness
in their sockets, and the absorption of the apices of the fangs, causing
constant tenderness, often extending to acute neuralgic symptoms.
The gums, in connection with these classes of teeth, are either of
extreme delicacy or of unusual thickness. The sockets—alveolar processes—are thin and spongiform in their texture, and through the
peculiarity of the periosteum of these and that of the succeeding group
of teeth, in a large number of instances, would seem to unite the teeth
and sockets, so that with difficulty they can be separated. It is of
frequent occurrence to detach portions of the sockets with the extracted teeth, and *no injury is done to the jaw,* although patients will
always insist that their jaws were broken.

The third of the classification of this group, the chalk-white teeth,
possess a uniform excess of lime constituent in their structure. Often
we observe, as if raised by an air-bubble beneath, small, half-developed
nodules of brown or yellowish lime deposit on the face of the enamel.
The teeth are brittle and soft in structure, and dry, that I have seen,
when well protected from the saliva—the *débris* of the excavated teeth
blown out as dry as the dust brushed from the chiseled marble. But
presently the instrument strikes upon a cartilaginous bone, covering
the nerve, and the same mistakes, in relation to supposed exposed

nerve-tissue, and the same results of intro-dental abscess, etc., attend them. From the same chemical causes affecting the previous teeth,—"white decay," softening of the bone into a chalky paste, and "crumbling away,"—disintegration of the teeth follows.

Usually, from the age of sixteen to thirty the teeth are affected by decay in pairs—right and left corresponding teeth; often by a general devastation. In none is this destruction of the ivory glory of the mouth more afflicting, in every sense of the word, than it is to girls of diathetic delicacy budding into womanhood—in the sunshine of loveliness and womanly beauty. It is indeed a loss that in youth's fleeting hour these beautiful organs should decay and die, leaving in their place their ill-conditioned or blackened remains, or their rankling "stumps," which, like dilapidated tombstones, present the sad *dento-memento mori* of all that was graceful, beautiful, and essential to the soul of expression, standing forth as they do in bold relief, a *festering contradiction*, proclaiming an undying opprobrium upon the false assertions of those who promise to make them last forever. They may exclaim with Macbeth,—

> " And be these juggling fiends no more believ'd,
> That palter with us in a double sense,
> That keep the word of promise to our ear
> And break it to our hope."

The wisdom teeth of this group, even before they make their appearance, in a large majority are very defective in their structure. Their removal demands much care and manipulative skill to avoid fracturing the inner plate of the alveoli of the lower jaw—an injury that inflicts weeks of misery and pain.

More irregularities of the teeth and malformations of the alveolar processes occur in this than in the previous groups of teeth. The bone-structure of the sockets in an eminent degree partakes of the characteristic structure of the teeth. They appear to obey peculiar physiological dynamics bearing on inferior organized bone, either by spreading *outward* the semicircumference of the alveolar circle, as might be represented by the projecting outline of the capital letter D, or by contracting *inward* the curvilineal circle like that of a small capital c—the outward-projecting curviform alveoli and teeth giving, as Mr. Darwin has it, an *"anthropomorphous"* or simeous type of expression to the jaws and mouth, while the contracted circle of the alveoli causes the teeth to be crowded into many and various deformities. Sometimes the upper teeth, alveoli, and maxilla protrude—"overhang" far outside of the lower teeth; while in others is seen the reverse order, the lower alveoli and teeth projecting and overshutting upon the upper teeth, and in others the back molar teeth, lengthened in both jaws, meeting before the front teeth can close upon each other, leaving a space between them, so that their incisory functions are prevented, as well as causing an imperfection in the enunciation of the voice.

With the exceptions hereafter mentioned, in these teeth we first have our attention attracted to the longitudinal lines of pitted indentations in the face-enamel of the teeth. They may be observed almost in the order or character of the diathesis of each individual. First one or two pits in each of the lower centre incisors. Sometimes the upper central incisors will be pitted with one indentation ; then we observe three pits in each of the four lower front teeth and two indentations in each of the superior incisors. In others we find three pits in the six lower front teeth and two pits in the six upper front teeth. In others a longitudinal line of imperfect indentations affects the whole—the two molars on either side excepted—of the lower teeth, and partially of the upper set of teeth. This peculiar malformation will be illustrated to its completion in the succeeding groups of teeth.

The dental student must not confound the occasional one or two slight indentations defacing the dense polished enamel of the first two groups as being identical with the dull, discolored, calcareous, deep pittings characterizing the weak, imperfect organization of the classes of the third and fourth groups of teeth. The indentations in the first two groups are caused by accidental, temporary interruption during the period of their formation, as in the second two groups the deficiency of proper material "nutrition," or perversion of secretion, may be traced almost step by step as *causæ evidentes*, or remote causes, of constitutional derangements in the animal economy produced by certain poisonous eruptive diseases—scarlet-fever, measles, smallpox, varioloid, etc.; and, alas! in too many instances their organization being in harmony with scrofulous, strumous, cancerous, and tuberculous diatheses of the several constitutions. In fact, the calcareous formations within the pits and in the substance of the teeth may be accepted as *dento-tuberculous* formations, and are the base of disease in teeth as much as tuberculous formations in the lungs are the basis of phthisis pulmonalis.

FOURTH GROUP. THE TRANSPARENT-WHITE ALABASTER TEETH. THE BLUE-WHITE PEARLY TEETH, AND THE TRANSPARENT-YELLOW TEETH WITH CLEAR EDGES.

With the fourth and last group, I conclude my remarks upon the notes of the pathology of my classification of the dental organs.

With unremitting zeal I have ever sought knowledge to base my treatment of the dental system upon correct medical and mechanical science. I have not failed to avail myself of the experience of others, from the most exalted to the lowliest in the profession. Indeed, some of my best lessons have been derived from the injurious practices of the latter.

I have respectfully and patiently listened to the experience of many dentists,—from some of whom, who have given wordy descriptions of their several individual modes of preserving the teeth forever, better things might have been expected than the display of their utter regardlessness of any knowledge or discrimination—I will not say pathology—of the physical varieties of the several densities of the teeth, and the *dissimilar strength* characterizing the multiform organization and construction of the enamel and bone tissues which, as mechanics, they should not have failed to recognize. Singular as this extraordinary oversight or omission of a remarkable existing vital physiological principle—always presenting itself—may appear, it is not so extraordinary under these adverse circumstances as the infallibility of their simple mechanical appliances, the inscrutability of which depends upon their individual magic of "doing it." A phenomenon that demands a recording page. But the record may with propriety ask the question, Why is Hippocrates more infallible than Herophilus, or Herophilus than Asclepiades, or his pupil Themiston, or Erasistratus, or Plistonicus, or his disciple Praxagoras?

We in our nature were always truthfully desirous of preserving the teeth of the many of the young and the beautiful who come under our professional care, some of whose very natures — affinity, spiritualists term it—imbue our sympathies with kindred affection, that all our zeal of friendly intention has concentrated our professional resource upon the one sincere object,—that of preserving and beautifying their teeth regardless of pecuniary reward. But, alas! hereditary predisposition, disease, malorganization, or premature decay is there, and we have not the principle of life in our power to renew or increase the vital force or improve it at our pleasure. The source of life and the causes of disease are hidden from our view. We can neither physiologically change, remove, nor restore a part of the body decayed and lost. We can interfere by our *nursing* offices with the action—whatever that may be—of Nature, through the influence of the general system, by general constitutional treatment, to improve the general health, and the temporary expedients of patching the decayed parts of teeth with gold, etc.; the duration of the latter depending upon the continued health of each individual, even in extreme delicate constitutions. It must be borne in mind that the derangements of the system, generally, do not consist in change of mechanical apposition, connection, or motion, which altogether control and constitute the derangements of a machine. Our organization is governed by invisible laws. Destitute, then, as we are of the powers and the information of the mechanist in this respect, we know that the diseases of any organ of the animal system are rarely the result of mechanical changes, and that our remedies do not act upon mechanical principles beyond the mere filling of decayed teeth mechanically. The future of professional observations opens an extended vista of leading points, viz., the discrimination of dento-pathological derangements, of dento-sympathetic affections; the anticipation of their changes and progress, and the indications of cure, and how these can be aided by the knowledge of anatomical, physiological, physical, and pathological scientific truth.

If I may be permitted to speak of my own experience, it has been the vital point of my existence to conquer or surmount never-ending difficulties. To this end I have served as surgeon in military hospitals in South America; as ship-surgeon: I faithfully fulfilled my time as assistant-surgeon in the New York Hospital, for which I received honorable certificates; I had the advantage of four years' office practice in the surgical department under the auspices of my much-esteemed preceptor the late distinguished surgeon Dr. John C. Cheesman; I served as assistant in the dental office of my father; in the same class with the now distinguished surgeons, James R. Wood, Carnochan, Worster, Alonzo Clark, and McReady, and with them I received medical honors from Mott, Stevens, Delafield, Torrey, John Augustine Smith, and others. With all this and forty years' practical experience, with unremitting attention, study, and observation, I have ever experienced that it is not possible to perform impossibilities; that no medical or mechanical Joshua exists that can command the laws of nature to stand still, or decay to retrograde. But I am told by an apothecary's clerk who graduated into being a dentist from selling cosmetics from behind a counter, that by his magic application of the mallet he can drive a piece of gold into a hole in a tooth and make it last forever!— not unlike the Egyptian of old, who advertised that his embalmed bodies should last ten thousand years or the money would be returned. I drew upon my bankers for two dollars, and paid for an annual membership in a dentist's society for mutual improvement. There I soon became acquainted with my own ignorance caused by misspent studies. As the Chinese philosophers sent a watchmaker to repair the steam-engine of a raised British war-steamer sunk by their guns before Peibo, so did similar philosophic mathematicians draw diagrams showing how nutrition was conveyed to the teeth, and how they are, or ought to be—on the blackboard—constructed and organized, and how simple it is to preserve them forever,—"a little sop of creasote," or "aconite," or "chloride of zinc," "placed in the cavities to obtund the sensitive dentine," and "fill over" with amalgam, or mallet in gold, and the thing is accomplished. This sort of dental science almost converted me into an uneasy state of skepticism. Believing that possibly a great mistake or oversight of omission had been made when man was created, I could not avoid philosophizing, why it was that a dentist's mutual improvement society—with a blackboard—was not first organized and consulted when Adam was teething. All then, indeed, would have been perfect. But the last, best, and admitted the most beautiful of creation—woman—Eve, being tempted, she inveigled Adam to use his teeth, by which he gained the terrible knowledge of the general doom,—that all created things must decay and die, not even omitting the teeth by which he ate of the forbidden apple. "But every one shall die for his iniquity; every man that eateth a sour grape, his teeth shall be set on edge," saith the Prophet Jeremiah.

To the schools I have already mentioned—certainly the best institutions of which the world can boast—must the student of the dentist's art look to become a well-informed, accomplished dentist. He will then discover that knowledge will raise him infinitely superior to his being "a mere tooth carpenter." In addition to this, he must not disregard the dictates of reason and reflection. His doctrines must be based upon good sense and sound philosophy. For a time, at least, he must ignore the egotistical "I am Sir Oracle." These will point out the true mode of investigating the phenomena of nature by unwearied experiments and watchfulness. The mode which Bacon labored to inculcate on the hypothesis-mongers of his age, which Newton successfully pursued, and which has hastened the philosophers of later times to the development of that fund of natural knowledge in the sciences of electricity, chemistry, mechanical, and every branch of natural philosophy by which modern inquiry is distinguished.

THE PATHOLOGY OF THE TEETH; A DELICATE CONSTITUTION! Can the brain of man or the libraries of the world enhance the impressive, comprehensive meaning and bearing contained in this brief sentence? From one extreme, of the light fragile mould of form, the classic-shaped head and lineaments of features, the well-"chiseled," dilating nostril, the fair, soft, smooth, transparent skin, the soft azure eye, sometimes beaming with an unearthly light, the long silken eyelashes, proudly curling, or meek, beauteous lips, pale, or deeply pinked, half concealing a "colonnade of pearls"; the delicate, clear, alabaster complexion, tinged with a roseate hue, the blue tendril veins marbling the temples, the even intelligent forehead; the small hand, with its tapering fingers and filbert-shaped nails, the "little feet," to the other extreme; the high, large, misshaped head, with compressed, flattened temples and large, rounded, projecting, overhanging forehead, with face small in proportion, narrow, deformed chest, flat or hollow at the sides, with projecting breast-bone, small, sharp, or large gray, soft, expressive eyes; tall and thin body, with ill-shaped limbs and large joints, curved spine, pale or white complexion, malshaped, irregular, mottled-colored or chalky-white teeth, large, or heavy, or tumid lips, etc.

A less common combination is a fair-proportioned figure, but with contracted thorax and narrow pelvis; expressive, and, oftentimes, beautiful features, large, soft, languid, or quick and brilliant black eyes, with deep, pearly sclerotica, full-developed vermilion-blooded lips; olive complexion, dark hair, and long black eyelashes; large regular or irregular teeth. The teeth, in their modifications of structure, form, and color, never failing to demonstrate, or rather offering an index exhibiting and marking each individual diathesis. The descriptive lines of Shakspeare say:

> "Till forging Nature be condemn'd of treason.
>   *   *   *   *
> And therefore hath she bribed the destinies
> And crossed the curious workmanship of Nature
> To mingle beauties with infirmities,
> And pure perfection with impure defeature,
>   Making it subject to the tyranny
>   Of sad mischance and much misery."

The full development of rounded beauty of the blonde, or that of the brunette, or the diversified features of each, denote the sero-lymphatic temperament, the strumous, the scorbutic, the tuberculous, and the cachectic predispositions. No matter how the physical appearance or how long a time it may represent the body in all the pride and confidence of health and beauty, the tell-tale teeth demonstrate the foundation of the peculiar diathetic characteristic of constitution inherited from parents and ancestors. *Well would it be for suffering humanity if the faculties of medical colleges, all over the world where medical science is taught, knew that this almost exact index exists as a diagnostic and pathognomonic mark of constitutional peculiarity.* Where these teeth are present, it will always be found, upon inquiry, that either on the father's or mother's side some had died of consumption, some of cancerous disease, some of glandular affections, some of malignant diseases, etc.

That *cachectic* predisposition may be fully understood. Its definition is—an "unhealthy" condition of the system. Allied to *anæmia*, it means a diminished quantity of red particles of the blood and its more solid ingredients; or, in other words, serous or watery blood. Its varieties inherited are tuberculous cachexia, cancerous cachexia, the cachexia (debility) of hot climates, marsh cachexia, syphilitic cachexia, and suprarenal (kidney) cachexia, or morbus Addisonii, etc.

The characteristics of the previous group apply to this classification of the fourth group of teeth, with the marked difference that gelatinous tissue predominates over the other constituents of the bone and enamel, bearing the comparative density and hardness with the first two groups as light, soft alabaster is to dense, obdurate granite.

These blue-white pearly teeth and the white teeth form the "colonnade of pearls," the "pearly gems," the "ivory portico," behind "coral lips," upon which the ideal of the poet dwells; form the lover's eulogy and the novelist's theme of facial expression, which everybody covets as the *beau ideal* of dental perfection and beauty. Unhappily they are the tell-tale signs of the hidden quicksands of danger beneath. They are but one remove from the structure and organization of the soft gelatinous formation of the first dentition, claiming a superiority because of their being larger, thicker, and better outlined and matured into adult feature.

Contrasting with these proverbially beautiful teeth, again we see how nature delights in the trick of producing opposites emanating from the same cause,—constitutional cachectic debility,—*i.e.* delicate constitution. The teeth present a disagreeable expression of lines, large, long, and ill-shaped teeth, and of a dirty, chalky color. The jaws and cheek-bones are hard and angular; large mouth, thick pale cold lips, and sallow complexion; eyes deeply seated within the protruding outline of the orbits, giving an expression as if death were peering through a living mask.

The indented formations in the enamel filled with lime accretions are many, and, unlike the dentings in the previous group, they are more irregular, and in some constitutions the teeth are almost separated into two parts—like the letter X—by a horizontal line of depression encircling each (the molars excepted) several tooth of the whole dental alignement. The cutting edges of the teeth are serrated with points and nodules of a mottled, dirty, chalky enamel. Sometimes these nodules are separated by the horizontal line denting the body of the teeth, the enamel of which presents a yellow-brown, or a white-greenish, uneven, noduled surface of partially crystallized lime. Oftentimes the enamel is entirely deficient upon the crowns of the molar teeth, which, on their masticating surfaces, present numerous small, enamel-discolored, denticulated points, as if artificially inserted into the denuded bone; or otherwise, with uneven, noduled surface. The disfigurement of the enamel is added to by the many malformations and irregularities of these teeth. They are eminently embarrassing to the dentist, as they are the cause of mortification and vexation to the feelings and pride of their possessors.

Their decay, almost at all times spontaneous, is hastened by the accidents of hysteria, chlorosis, epilepsy,—fearfully on the increase,—dyspepsia, gestation, lactation, too much confinement in-doors, alcoholic cachexia, anxiety, grief, overwork, want of proper (suitable) nutritious food, etc., in adults. In children, supermental exertion, studies, absence of *instinctive*, cheerful recreations in the sunshine abroad. In youth, dissipations, smoking, tight-lacing, and, above all, the absence of respiring the BREATH OF LIFE in the free, open, pure, nutritive air, which electro-vivifies, oxygenates, and supplies the electro-vital-nervous force to develop and sustain every atom of the animal organization.

In many, the cachectic pathology of the teeth is of a character that the mere examining them superinduces a "nervous" effect, not only upon the mind, but upon the teeth and upon the whole body, causing great prostration, and, in two cases which came under my notice, a state of collapse. To meddle with them is torture; to leave them alone insures their speedy decay. The only method of reaching them is by judicious constitutional and local treatment and rational nursing.

Goldsmith's "Citizen of the World" says, "How foolish it is to be sick, how silly it is to die!" When all we have to do is to read newspaper advertisements, where we can learn how to be healed and live forever. With the advance of the knowledge of natural philosophy, *pro rata* strides are made with philosophic nonsense. Lord Byron dieted on fish, chiefly, believing that fish recuperated his brain with phosphorus derived from this diet; since which time Byron's crochet has been adopted as a physiological truth. We cannot make *red blood* from fish diet, hence Byron had bad teeth, and he died early of debility, relapsing fever, or typhoid—it is the same.

On the south and east end of Long Island cachectic depravity of the blood is actually—though unintentionally—cultivated. This part of the island is manured with fish taken from the neighboring waters. The malaria of phosphorus poisons eliminated from the putrescent land renders the population fishy,—cachectic,—their teeth fishy too, decaying early and rapidly. Fevers are endemic.

The small island on the western side of St. Eustatius—one of the West India Islands—called the isle of *Saba*, was originally peopled by a stalwart, healthy, hardy race of Scots. These people, through each succeeding generation, have subsisted exclusively on fish diet. In these people we have the illustration and demonstration how blood and habit of body may be deteriorated, while the organizations are forever the same, however inferior. In this way the functions of nature may be diversified into individual diathesis, but natural organization cannot be permanently altered, although sometimes we read of monstrosities, and even see "freaks of Nature." The "New Theory in Dental Histology," by S. P. Cutler, M.D., D.D.S., published in the DENTAL COSMOS, vol. xiii., No. 3, page 121, cannot be sustained in this particular. From the time of Isaac, circumcision has been practiced upon millions upon millions, through a period of nearly four thousand years, or one hundred and seventy generations; yet we find *nature reigns supreme;* and so with the Chinese practice of diminishing the feet for many generations. Bad blood—the result of "sin," of climate, or accident, or whatever it may be—is sometimes inherited; that we know,—it proves nothing more.

The fish-fed *Sabans* present a people of decrepitude, premature old age, scorbutic, and of *leprous* diathesis. Their bodies are hideously disgusting, being covered with desquamating skin in the shape of large scales. Their fingers and toes ulcerate away, joint after joint, leaving mere stumps. Their teeth are thin, clear, gelatinous, and fish-like in every particular, only that they are shaped, featured, and outlined as human teeth. They are affected by all the peculiarities attending tuberculous or scrofulous teeth. It cannot be said of them that they decay. They cave in, "crumble in," or melt away, as a sand-bank is washed down by soft rains. The act of eating or drinking is their torture, and, finally, when their crowns are wasted away, soft, pasty fangs, of almost diffused nervous matter, with constant neuralgic pains, remain to distress the unfortunate sufferers. The curious phenomenon of atavism is here fully established. Almost in every family the affection has been observed to miss a generation, in which the original good teeth will be present, and the bad teeth surely reappearing in the succeeding one. The people on the opposite land, only eight miles distant, living generously and naturally, possess teeth of the ordinary excellence in common with the generality of the dental organs of other well-developed, well-fed people.

The distinguished cook, Professor Blot, says in a lecture "On Cooking as an Art," delivered at the Cooper Institute, "you cannot make a gentleman by feeding him on codfish;" which may be interpreted, that fishy *white* blood, and a *white liver* are incompatible with the warm manners characterizing the presence of *red* blood. The professor says that "food is the most important of our wants, as we cannot exist without it," which nobody can deny. "If one has mental labor, fish"—shade of Byron!—"should be eaten every other day," AND "fish and cheese are the best articles of diet for children." Persons that cannot swim should not wade beyond their depth. The professor may cook a fish to perfection, or transform a piece of cheese into a Welsh-"rabbit"—rarebit—but he must not blot out our children with such a diet as his cookery recommends. Our children's teeth are fishy and cheesy enough without assisting the *swill* and *condensed* milk diet to increase the ill-definable debility of their dental organs, already sufficiently embarrassing to the professional dentist. A natural diet and a mother's care are demanded to secure health and good teeth. Dr. Willard Parker, our distinguished surgeon, speaking upon the "Reorganization of the New York Infant Asylum," says, "that at an asylum in Montreal, where children were artificially fed, out of 4059 children received in six years, 3767 died, or 93 per cent. At Randall's Island, New York, but ten out of every hundred lived, and where nurses were provided $27\frac{1}{2}$ per cent. lived, and where the *mother* cared for the child full 70 per cent. lived." The great chemist, Liebig, proposed an artificial food for children. It was tried in the Paris hospitals. The result was that children survived on the experiment three and four days only.

Thus it ever will be. The egotism of theorists, based upon scientific ingenuity, leads them into the belief that they can condense nature into the limits of a nutshell; and, while they are imposing upon themselves and leading an "enlightened public" into the most serious of unphilosophical errors, practical experience demonstrates that we cannot violate the mathematical laws of the vital forces of nature without paying a severe penalty. Nor can we govern the dynamics influencing vitality and organization. All human chemical knowledge *may* propose, but nature *will dispose*.

Dr. J. W. McCormick, M.R.C.S., British army, E. I., describes, in *The Transactions of the Medical and Physical Journal of Calcutta*, many interesting cases of dental affections superinduced by bad diet, exposure, and debility of the stomach, or gastric irritations; and this, too, among the British troops, selected, "picked" men, wherein "puffy, spongy, hemorrhagic, vegetating, painful gums were present, and the teeth 'crumbled away' or perpendicularly split in two."

The gums embracing the teeth in health are thin, compact, and either pale, or of a peach-blossom or a delicate pink-salmon color. In their reverse order they are thick, flabby, tumid, turgescent, spongy, and flaccidly connected with the necks of the teeth. The teeth, too, speedily disintegrate or break off, leaving painful, festering stumps, suppurating gums, and irritable canker ulcers upon the whole mucous membrane of the mouth, and often extending into the throat and bronchial tubes. Mothers during the nursing period frequently suffer much from these tuberculous canker sores.

To what extent the pathological condition of the teeth, in whatever original constitutional diathesis they may be, is affected by vaccine matter or *virus* taken from strumous or scorbutic children, the offspring of phthisical or consumptive parents, and indiscriminately introduced into the systems of children free from hereditary taint in their blood, remains to be demonstrated or disproven—whether the correctness of my hypothesis upon this point be what I deem it to be, the cause of another pathological condition of the teeth.

Internal decay in the first and second groups I have rarely met with; in the gelatinous class of the third group occasionally; but in the classes of this fourth group it is of common occurrence. The internal disease, in fact, is the original defective secretion, deposit, organization, solidification, and imperfect ossification, of the teeth, which are almost cartilaginous in their texture; they present gelatinous matter, saturated, as it were, with solidified lime from a gristly bone solution, and covered with a delicate, translucent, imperfectly-crystallized enamel. In the centre of the substance of these teeth may be seen a deep-seated blue spot like a diminutive bruise spot, which, examined by the aid of the microscope, exhibits tuberculous tissue. We find the germs of malignant disease in the organization of the teeth as well as in the lungs and in other organs of the body. In the case of Mr. ——, one of the editorial staff of the *New York Herald*, who died of what is termed "galloping consumption," the teeth were of surpassing beauty, in size, shape, form, and regularity; but all were affected by this internal, tuberculous, malignant disease. The action of the disease was so rapid, that three weeks from the time of his "taking his death of cold," the sockets of the teeth and the gum portions of the jaw-bones were entirely denuded of their investing covering—the gums. They had suppurated and melted away, leaving the livid lips with the terrible expression of a living, grinning skeleton beneath. The majority of the teeth quickly crumbled into pieces or suddenly caved in before his death.

In all anæmic systems the teeth are sympathetically affected by local or constitutional irritation, and the teeth reciprocate the compliment by exciting constitutional and remote symptoms of neuralgic troubles.

The wisdom teeth are nearly always incomplete in constructive organization, and often are little better than agglomerated matter. If any wisdom be furnished by their eruption, the suggestion would be, have them "out" as soon as possible.

The teeth! By dentists looked upon as furnishing articles of trade and profit; by their possessors, as ornament of pearl, to complete the perfection of the "human face divine;" by anatomists and physiologists—pathologists, they have none to befriend them,—as necessary mechanical triturating instruments.

The teeth! Have they no higher—important as it is—grade than their being mere "grinders" and "incisors?" We have been told, and it has been published too, what a capital thing it is to those afflicted with *"congenital cleft palate,"* that by their malformation they can effectually acquire the *nasal twang* necessary to speak the *French* language with native excellence. But of the physiological character of the teeth, as connected and identified with the vocal powers of enunciation, pronunciation, intonation, emphasis, and modulating and articulating sounds, we have never been told; that the teeth are the great conservators of the lungs, we have never been told; that by their adaptation they permit the breath of life to pass into the lungs by a slow and natural force suitable to the gradual inflation and expansion of the organs of respiration; that they act as a dam, preventing the too sudden emptying of the mouth, and consequently the exhaustive use of too large a column of breath to be expired through the larynx from the lungs at each expiration, or by each act of speaking, thereby preventing repetitions of sudden collapses of the organs of respiration and the consequent exhaustion of the nerves of respiration. In ordinary speaking, reading, singing, preaching, haranguing, the teeth never permit an atom more of breath to be expended from the lungs than is mathematically required to enunciate each separate sound through the aperture of the teeth. By the absence of the teeth, each enunciation of vocal sound causes the breath contained in the mouth to be expended at once, and which is replaced with each renewed enunciation by *per saltum* jerks, as it were, of breath from the lungs—causing a sensation of weakness in the chest, and pain in the side, short breath, *dyspnœa*, and "dry cough," followed by general exhaustion. Under such circumstances the "old folks" lie down or sit melancholy and moping away in their arm-chair, and the young folks take cod-liver oil and iron, apply plasters and take change of air, *secundum artem*. With infants, crying and "crowing" answer the purpose of speaking, singing, and haranguing, as exercises to the muscles of respiration.

The miseries attending the absence of the teeth from the mouth are often increased by the too frequent and oftentimes unnecessary removal of the tonsils from the "throat;" organs whose physiological intentions are to modify the temperature of the atmosphere inhaled into the lungs, and to protect and warm the *epiglottis* and its *rima-glottidis*, and by their secreted fluid to lubricate the parts forming the entrance into the larynx or windpipe.

During the period of the last forty years I have retained several families, their children and their grandchildren, all differing in constitutional habit of body, whose dental systems have been under my professional supervision and care, which, with the experience derived under similar circumstances among many other families, although of not so long duration of time, yet still of sufficient lengths of periods to enable me to recognize analogous pathological conditions of the teeth, and to analyze the cause of their differences under the several peculiar adverse constitutional circumstances distinguishing them. By these fortunate circumstances I am enabled to throw my observations together in the condensed form of these "notes." I deem their accuracy to be of sufficient importance to offer them to my professional brethren as a guide, or a starting-point, for us to unite in the one object of pursuing the subject to its complete development; that, by our united experience and observations, we may ultimately secure a perfect dental science, and the distinguished position that such a science has the right to demand among the practitioners and professors of the healing art.

From my long practical experience, the gratification of my professional pride is being able to state that in the several families in which I have been professionally retained for so many years, *I have filled as few teeth as possible*. This practice has not been *profitable financially*, but it is conservative, and above all it is professional. I have relied upon constitutional and conservative treatment, which have been the means of conserving the teeth to their owners for much longer periods than would *too much* mechanical officiousness in filling natural fissures that rarely ever decay.

Of the very many cases treated constitutionally with success, the following will point a moral and adorn my history :

Miss ——, a beautiful young lady, aged twenty years, of sero-lymphatic temperament, and constitutionally anæmic, was placed under my professional care at the age of ten years. Her teeth were soft, full of indentations, and were covered with a mottled-colored, yellow-brown, muddy accretion of lime enamel. I furnished her with a special dentifrice, for the purpose of rubbing away this disfiguring surface of the teeth, hoping to come to a substratum of good enamel. I did not fail to impress upon her mind that continued good health—for the weakly can be "healthy"—was necessary to effect the success of our undertaking, which must be assisted by her own constant attention, and by persistently observing the directions given to her, when, *perhaps*, "after five years or so," a good enamel might be exposed. She was an intelligent child, and ambitious. Aided by the constant watching of her constitutional health by the family physician, the distinguished Dr. Gesheidt, our efforts were crowned with complete success. If there was ever a case of abnormal condition, where nature, untiring and persistent personal attention and professional honesty, deserved credit and unqualified recognition for its complete success, our united efforts claimed and deserved it.

Here we have a perfect illustration how anæmic teeth, in delicate constitutions, may be conserved by judicious constitutional care, local treatment, and strict attention.

DENTO-NEURALGIA.

Apart from the mechanical appliances for the conservation of the teeth, the course of proceeding in learning the disease of the dental system necessarily must be the same as pertains to obtaining a knowledge of the disease of the organs of hearing and of the organs of vision, which must be based upon the sciences of anatomy, physiology, pathology, and therapeutics, with the difference of peculiarity in relation to the teeth, which, as I have demonstrated, present several constitutional varieties in the densities of their structure, both in their bone and enamel organization.

With very few exceptions, the causes of neuralgia are involved in the deepest obscurity. The subject, to be appreciated, must be studied from the beginning of the sciences bearing upon the animal organization. The nervous system is the "box of tools" by which Nature performs her work. Dento-neuralgia connects the fifth, sixth, seventh, eighth, ninth, tenth pairs and the cervico-spinal nerves. These nerves, of course, are correlated with the other nerves of the system.

Of the several divisions into which the general pathology of the human system is divided, not one of them has been passed over with less observation than the pathology of the dental nerves in their connection with the dental organs and the regions of the face, head, neck, shoulders, arms, hands, and fingers, and their neuralgic-sympathetic influences upon the remote organs of the body.

The little knowledge possessed, and the limited information furnished,—for the disease itself, like many other nervous disorders, is based upon speculation,—relative to its cause and nature, and the treatment indicated, has amounted to nothing that offers any specific guide either for its amelioration or cure. Now and then hospital clinics exhibit a case of neuralgia produced by morbid lesions or the accidents of surgery, which, so far from throwing any light upon the subject, or even affording an insight by which a treatment for its cure might be adopted, the faculty, remaining at fault, are compelled to allow it to take its place with many incurable diseases, which furnish an opprobrium upon the science of medicine.

This circumstance is more to be regretted, because dentists have many opportunities, of cases which daily present themselves to their notice, whereby to investigate the subject. That these advantages should pass unheeded and *unknown*, must be attributed to the mechanical eagerness for a superior reputation in "tooth-filling," and the fabulous fees to be obtained therefor, in preference to any natural philosophy "that does not pay." What good might not be accomplished by the thousands of dental practitioners overflowing every large city, flooding every small town, and crowding every village, nook, and corner of this vast, wide-spread country,—and "the cry is still they come,"—were they not influenced more by money-making motives than by a wish to exalt the character of dento-medico science in its correlation with medical science!

If the dental profession have failed to observe these constant and almost universal pathological neuralgic affections, the reason is obvious, and the truth must be told. It is because the dental profession, with a very few distinguished exceptions, are devoid of anatomical, physiological, and pathological requirements and knowledge to enable them to see the phenomena every day passing before their eyes. If the medical practitioner has failed to recognize or even to make the acquaintance of dento-cause and sympathetic effect relative to the many dento-neuralgic sympathies constantly passing under his notice, it is because he is equally ignorant of dento-neuralgic phenomena, for he has neglected the study of this branch system of anatomy, physiology, and pathology of the dental organization, as being unnecessary, too trivial, and beneath the dignity of his far-reaching learning. If the "tooth-carpenter" *cannot*, certainly the *physician* ought to appreciate the fact that the organs of the body cannot be comprehended as a whole unless each organ and system be well understood as to their individual intention, with their wide-spread influence and intimate connection, as well as their mutual dependence and direct sympathy with each other.

THE WONDERFUL NERVOUS SYSTEM!—the physical representative of the more wonderful VITAL principle or force which endows every atom of the body, including the blood, with active properties or functions; the instruments by which each several atom of each several organization is guided or moulded into the form of the various systems, and united into one harmonious whole, which by sensibility warns of danger, which gives expression and furnishes motive power, which combats external agents and preserves the being,—the phenomena of which are recognized, but they are beyond the power of the human mind to explain. The exhaustion of the nervous force is repaired by sleep, and the involuntary "vital organs," such as the heart, lungs, muscles of respiration, etc., by *repose*. The irritation of a nerve of sensation causes pain; of a nerve of motion, muscular contraction; of the nerve of the *retina*, the sensation of light; of the auditory nerve, the sensation of sound; of the origin of the pneumogastric nerve, a derangement of the digestive process, with all the concomitant symptoms of dyspepsia, etc. Then the *reflex* action of the nervous fibres of one part reacting upon another part of the body,—such as the irritation of the nose, causing a spasm of the great muscle of respiration, the diaphragm; the effect, sneezing. The inflammation of the parotid glands, "mumps," being replaced in the breast, or testes, and *vice versa*, retrocedent. Gout and rheumatism of the joints, by *metastasis*, changing their place to the kidneys, stomach, heart, etc. Erysipelatous inflammation "striking" into the brain. Certain sounds irritating the auditory nerves, and through them to the dental fifth pair of nerves, putting "the teeth on edge," and causing a thrill throughout the nervous system, known as "making the blood run cold." A tumor on a nerve produces twitchings and spasms in parts totally remote and unconnected with the origin. Some pathologists apply to these nervous phenomena "radiation of sensation." Persons deprived of an arm or a leg, for the rest of their lives occasionally experience pains, tingling, or pricking sensations, as if the limbs were still present; the cicatrized nerves of the "stumps" being irritated from cause, convey to the brain their pain by a false impression, as if they were entire, and still extended their sentient fibrils to the fingers or toes. A blow on the head affects the stomach, causing vomiting, etc., and a blow on the stomach, by reflex action of the eighth pair of nerves, in pugilist's parlance, "doubles a man up," and a more violent blow, the *coup de grace*, the blow of mercy of ancient torture, causes instant death, paralyzing the stomach, and hence the brain. The sensations of creeping insects, reptiles, etc., affecting delirium tremens patients, are the results of reflex action of the debilitated, perverted gastric sentient nerves of the stomach upon the sensorium, and thence to the nerve fibres, spreading themselves throughout the skin.

Nosologists classify neuralgic nerve-pain affections according to the name of the region in which the pain is experienced. Thus, *neuralgia faciei*, nerveache of the face, the *tic convulsif* and *tic douloureux* of the French; *neuralgia policis, neuralgia pedis*, of the foot; *otalgia*, earache; *neuralgia mamma*, of the breasts; the *ischias nervosum*, or pain in the great sciatic nerve; disease of the hip-joint, pain in the knee, odontalgia, toothache, etc.

Of the little that is known of neuralgia, that of dento-neuralgia is altogether lost sight of, although scarcely a day passes without it being presented in some shape to the dentist and physician. Many regions of the body receive the credit of its presence by the several local nomenclature by which they are recognized, but to which, in very numerous instances, they have neither claim nor title; they are sympathetic in character only, and are found to originate in the abnormal condition of the dental organs where no apparent pain is experienced, and where the cause is rarely if ever suspected. To these sympathetic dento-neuralgic affections my "notes" refer, and not to ordinary odontalgic pains in the teeth and gums alone, which diagnostically speak for themselves.

Harris's Dictionary of Dental Science, with all the zealous research of the accomplished author, condenses all that is known of neuralgia in the definition and history of *odontalgia*. Mr. Thomas Bell, London, says "it not unfrequently happens that parts most remote become the seat of pain from exposure of the nerve of a tooth;" but here we are furnished with a diagnostic mark. Dr. Good, in his great work, does not refer to the dental system; he says that "neuralgia is often an idiopathic (self-generated) affection, dependent upon a peculiar irritation from a cause we cannot trace. But," continues the doctor, "it is more frequently a *disease of sympathy*, produced by pregnancy, chronic rheumatism, or acrimony of the stomach." Dr. Wood refers to odontalgic affections where the disease is marked by pain in the teeth themselves, ordinary "toothache, with darting pains to the ear." Dr. Thomas E. Bond, in his *Treatise on Dental Medicine, etc.*, under the caption of "Neuralgia," remarks: "The term neuralgia is not precise, but it is sufficient for practical distinction. It is not certain," he says, "whether the seat of the disease is in the neurilemma or in the nervous pulp" (of the tooth). Dr. Bond pertinently says: "It will be perceived at once that the dentist must be called upon to discriminate between the disease and an ordinary toothache, and unless he be properly informed on these subjects, he may add to the terrible sufferings of his too confiding patients." Upon this hint the doctor rests.

The "singular" cases recorded, at periods remote from each other, of neuralgia disappearing *immediately* after the removal of a diseased tooth, are not so remarkable as the singular neglect of the circumstances presenting themselves, and that such marked and valuable hints should ever have incited an inquiry or philosophical investigation, why or how, or under what pathological circumstances, such supposed serious complaints were so quickly, easily, and completely removed, and why *such* singular cases should have produced no other impression upon the mind of the medical practitioner than that of being mere curiosities of pathological phenomena.

The following interesting cases, recorded by such distinguished men, certainly ought to have awakened attention, and moved the mind to their investigation. The great Dr. Rush records a case of "madness occasioned by diseased teeth, *which were in no ways painful to the patient,*" and recovery after their removal. Dr. Rush also states a case of HIP-JOINT DISEASE and rheumatic affection being *immediately removed* after the extraction of a tooth. The *London Lancet* records a case of "neuralgia of the womb *immediately disappearing* after the extraction of a diseased wisdom tooth." The celebrated Koecker, of Philadelphia, relates a case of epilepsy at once disappearing after the extraction of some diseased teeth. I could fill a volume of dento-neuralgic cases thus sympathetically affecting remote regions of the body, which were immediately cured by the removal of teeth in which disease or the cause of the sympathy was never suspected.

The following selected important cases will indorse the above, sufficiently to prove the correlation of dento-neuralgia with the sympathies of remote organs: The late Dr. John Wheeler, of this city, had *gout-podagra* and rheumatic affection in his right foot and leg for several years, which immediately disappeared after the extraction of the right anterior inferior molar tooth, which had been poisoned by arsenic placed in the tooth to destroy the nerve; five years later, lameness from rheumatic affection in the left *gastrocnemius*, or great muscle of the calf of the leg, immediately disappearing after the removal of the left molar tooth, which pained him from a cold "caught" while fishing.

Mrs. D., neuralgia in throat, neck, and shoulders; at intervals; nine years' standing. Dr. McComb recommended her to consult me. I removed the right central tooth of the lower jaw; tooth apparently sound in every respect; but atrophied at the root, its apex absorbed, and the end of the fang spiculated. Neuralgia did not reappear.

Mr. Dubois, New Rochelle, neuralgia in the stomach; sufferings intense. At the time of the first series of paroxysms I extracted the lower right central incisor; neuralgia cured for several months. On a second series of attacks I removed the lower left central incisor. Relief was instantaneous, and the neuralgia never reappeared.

Mr. McMinn, of Memphis, had traveled Europe for the best advice; "spent a fortune" and derived no benefit. He called upon me to have some artificial teeth repaired, and related his "years of suffering." I pointed out to him that every remaining tooth in his head was *dead*, and that all the neuralgic and paralytic symptoms in his arms, fingers, and toes, benumbed and pricking sensations, and the rheumatic pains in the *intercostal* muscles (some of the muscles of respiration), causing dyspnœa, or difficulty of breathing, were the sympathetic nervous results of his deranged and irritated dental nerves caused by the teeth being dead, etc. After mature consideration, never having experienced any pain in his teeth, he consented to have them all removed. The relief was *immediate* and *permanent*. The teeth were remarkable for their enormous size and dry, glassy brittleness.

Miss G., aged twenty-one; affected with *epileptic fits* since she was seventeen years of age. She had all sorts of treatment; went South, to Havana, to Europe; no beneficial results. After two years' persuading, she submitted to have the two lower wisdom teeth cut down upon and extracted; cure permanent.

Mr. H., a neighbor, seventy-five years old, suffered from *hemicrania* and *tic douloureux*, extending to the right eyeball. For a period of three years, in which time he completely lost the sight of the eye, he was "teased" by his niece to consult me. He was a rough old man; he wanted to know, "What can a *dentist* tell about these things, when all the surgeons who have examined my mouth say there is nothing the matter with it?" I had informed him that all his pains were caused by *spiculated* remains of fangs remaining beneath the gums, and were in process of being absorbed; hence the irritation of the dental nerves and their sympathetic irritations in the scalp, face, and eye. Finally, his sufferings were so acute that they compelled him to request me to examine his mouth again. * * * I cut down upon the upper jaw-bone, and took away three pinhead-sized spiculated ends of fangs. The operation caused the most excruciating agony, which I had fortunately foretold him. It is a singular circumstance attending the removal of these dento-causes of neuralgic affections, that the *after-pain* is of the most intense character, and lasts from ten minutes to *ten hours*, for which the operator gets not only the credit of being a magnificent bungler, but the "blessings" also of the indignant patient. Indeed, the dentist himself, like the patient, not being cognizant of this peculiar attending symptom, has his own confidential doubts upon the subject. From the time of the removal of the three spiculæ, now ten years, Mr. H. has never experienced a returning neuralgic symptom.

The niece of this gentleman and the daughter of Judge H., of Long Island, a beautiful girl, nineteen years of age, had been for several years "a martyr to neuralgic headaches"—*hemicrania*. She was "pa's pet." Judge H. insisted upon paying me ten thousand dollars if I could cure "pa's pet." I did effect a perfect and permanent cure for pa's pet by removing two teeth apparently sound, and filling two decaying teeth with gold. The judge "could not understand such a mode of procedure;" which showed that he was no judge in matters above his comprehension. "Pa" never paid me that ten thousand dollars, nor the first cent of a fee; and in addition he obtained an artificial set of teeth for his "dear"—to me—"wife."

Miss McC. had one superior central tooth remaining in her jaw. Artificial teeth replaced the lost teeth on both jaws; she was much annoyed by being "laughed at by her friends for a gouty old maid." Her foot and toe for a long time had been much swollen and very painful. She consulted me in relation to a constant slight *tickling* sensation at the root of the tooth, and at times a simultaneous throbbing in the tooth, with the pain-throbs in the toe-joint. I informed her that I was of opinion that the tooth was the original cause of her sympathetically affected gouty foot, but that I would not be positive on the point, as the crown and neck of the tooth and the gums also were both beautiful and sound in appearance. I struck the tooth a smart blow with a steel hammer, without producing any symptom. I applied a piece of zinc and silver to the neck of the tooth; a sharp, tingling shock was produced at

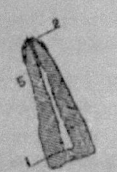

the root and a simultaneous darting pain in the foot. I extracted the tooth. The apex of the fang (see cut of the split tooth) was spiculated with needle-like points, embraced by a small sac filled with fetid matter. The pain in the foot subsided within an hour and has not reappeared since,— twelve years.

1. Chamber of tooth filled with fetid pus.
2. Spiculated apex and sac of pus.
5. Side of fang partially atrophied.

These cases sufficiently illustrate the dento-neuralgic sympathetic affections, *wherein no warning diagnostic mark or symptom is experienced by the patients themselves to induce a suspicion that the dental organs are the exciting cause.*

Dento-neuralgic sympathetic affections appear in their greatest frequency, commencing with the wisdom teeth and proceeding, as near as I can form a table of causes, in their order here enumerated. The wisdom teeth, first, being the exciting cause seven times to one of the second enumerated cause, and so on, until they are affected as five hundred times to once of the thirteenth enumerated cause. Being confined to a limited space, I am compelled to relinquish the completion of my notes upon dento-neuralgic sympathies of the remote regions of the body, and confine my remarks to the immediate localities of the face, the forehead, the head, the neck, shoulders, arms, hands, and fingers, where the sympathetic affections of the teeth are most likely to be recognized by the practicing dentist.

TABLE OF EXCITING CAUSES OF DENTO-NEURALGIC SYMPATHETIC AFFECTIONS.

1st. Diseased wisdom teeth, and teething excitement when making their "*eruption.*"

2d. The absorption of the gelatinous tissue from the bone of the fangs, leaving their surface rough and the ends of the fangs sharp and spiculated.

3d. The absorption of the dental sockets,—alveolar processes,—and by their covering gums being receded *below* the necks of the teeth, and below the bifurcation-separation of the fangs of the bicuspids and molar teeth. Being deprived of the natural nutritive, warming, protecting covering of the gums, the whole nervo-dental system is influenced—irritated—by numerous external agents, more especially those of atmospheric influences, causing neuralgic-rheumatic affection of face, neck, back of the head and shoulders, etc.

4th. Atrophy, or wasting of the fangs of the teeth, and the gradual death of the fangs, leaving spiculated apexes, or points.

5th. Abrasion, and exposure of the necks of the teeth.

6th. Injuries done by arsenious acid, aconite, chloride of zinc, carbolic acid, etc., when accidentally or imprudently used beyond the vital force of the teeth.

7th. Constitutional irritations, and those caused by mercury, iron, iodine, arsenic, quinine, etc., when used to excess.

8th. Electro-galvanic action of compound metals filled into teeth ; and the electro-galvanic action of alloyed metals used in soldering platina, gold, and silver plates, and soldering artificial teeth to such plates, by badly alloyed solders.

9th. The dead, poisonous matter of decomposed nerves confined within the chambers of the teeth.

10th. The too rapid wearing down of the crowns of the teeth, not permitting the nerves sufficient time naturally to recede.

11th. The dead roots or fangs of teeth, spiculated by the action of the absorbents.

12th. Hypertrophy or enlargement of the fangs, and the consequent absorption of the alveoli, causing nerve irritation.

13th. The absence of the teeth, causing an unnatural closing of the jaws and an overshutting of the joints upon their sockets, as a door strained by overshutting upon its hinges, irritating the third branch of the fifth pair of nerves.

14th. By deep "air-chambers" applied to plates for artificial teeth for the purpose of increasing the atmospheric pressure upon them, by which a constant irritation is produced upon B C and fig. 1, Plate I.—the filaments of the second branch of the fifth pair of nerves spread through the roof of the mouth.

These are some of the exciting causes by which the essential points for the basis of a correct diagnosis of the many pains and rheums appearing without any other apparent cause may be recognized, and which, as I have demonstrated, are dependent upon and arising from a source hitherto entirely overlooked. I can cite many cases in which patients, for years, have been subjected to the most harassing and distressing treatments,—narcotics, stimulants, sedatives, irritants, and counter-irritants, "nervines," carbonates, phosphates, acids, alkalies, tonics, iron, arsenic, mercury, quinine, phlebotomy, cupping and leeching, drastic alteratives and aperients, cold and warm, sulphur and vapor, Russian and Turkish baths, and sea-bathing, Sharon and other springs, electricity, the knife, the division and *excision* of the nerve; then homœopathy, hydropathy, "water-cure;" then mesmerism, spiritualism, clairvoyance, quack medicines, and the kindred sciences, have in their turns promised to effect a certain cure. If the wretched sufferer has had vital force sufficient to endure and withstand these dreadful assaults upon his poor frail citadel of flesh and blood, so wonderfully made and so resistingly combined, it has been to sink into a state of apathetic melancholy or hopeless despair. In many instances, as I have shown, the tortured patients, at last, have been relieved and cured of their misery by the removal of diseased wisdom teeth or spiculæ of fangs hidden beneath the gums.

The three accompanying plates furnish maps of the outlines of the great fifth pair of nerves, a portion of the seventh pair, and the cervical or neck nerves, and their several most important branches, without enlarging upon their increasing numerous offshoots and anastomosing-communicating filaments conjoining with other equally important nerves. They are introduced here for the purpose of demonstrating the sympathetic points and the relative positions of neuralgic symptoms, pains in the integuments of the jaw, head, neck, etc. For example, letter C, Plate I., represents the nerve of the upper wisdom tooth; the tooth is the cause of the nerve irritation; the *pain is not experienced in the wisdom tooth itself*, but, like the distribution of an electric wire, it is distributed to the other extremity or extremities, at some of the extreme branches, the sentient filaments of the nerves to the eye and nose (see fig. 3, 3, 3), or to the various other points on the forehead, temple, face, ear, back of the head, to the throat, chin, etc. figured in Plate III. Again, letter C, Plate I., the nerve of the wisdom tooth is in a state of irritation, and no pain has ever been experienced in the tooth to cause a suspicion that it is defective or affected, but pain is felt in the nerves of the teeth between it and the front teeth at letter B. At this moment of writing I have just extracted a wisdom tooth from the mouth of a lady friend, who has lost the two bicuspid teeth and a molar tooth, which were sound and perfect in every respect, but supposed to be defective, because in them was the apparent seat of pain. I had a quarrel with the patient on this point, she insisting that the molar sound tooth was the offending cause, until I passed an instrument into the nerve of the wisdom tooth and *convinced* her to the contrary.

Dento-neuralgia affects any *one* of these remote points of nerves sympathetically, or any *number* of them, or all of them together, according with each peculiar neuralgic affection. Sometimes it is "rheumatism" in the jaws, at other times in the face, again over the scalp, in the neck—"stiff neck;" rheumatism in the shoulders, in the arms, hands, fingers, etc., often attended with numbness, pricking sensations, as if the hand or arm were "asleep," creeping sensations upon the skin, as if insects were crawling, or a piece of silk thread or a cobweb were adhering to the skin; *pain in the eye, muscæ volitantes,* or motes, or rings, or disks floating before the eye ; pain in the temple, in the ear, and upon the apex of the head, etc. The dento-neuralgic symptoms thus extend their impressions to all parts of the body.

The most frequent neuralgic sympathetic pain is in the temporal region, in the eye, in the ear, and upon the crown of the head, arising from a diseased wisdom tooth on that side of the head where the pain is experienced. The pain is also sympathetically experienced in the *sound* teeth anterior to the affected wisdom tooth, which is in no way suspected of being the offending cause in any of these sympathetic symptoms. Thousands of sound teeth are thus sacrificed without any real cause. I have many contentions with patients upon this point. They want me to extract or to treat sound teeth as the offending organs, and when I inform them that they are mistaken, they look at me in wonderment, and often ask me if I take them "for fools" or "simpletons," that *they* cannot tell, and that they do not know where and in which tooth they feel the pain. Of course I am the victor in the end.

Thirty-five years ago my attention was attracted to dento-neuralgic sympathetic pains occurring in remote parts of the body. I have since devoted all the attention that time and opportunity would afford to glean such data as would elucidate the subject, and the proper treatment for their cure. The results of my investigations have been many, the details of which my limited space prevents me entering upon; one of which, however, will be found of great practical use to the surgeon dentist. *It is the obtunding or benumbing the extremities of the temporal nerves for painless extraction of teeth from their sockets* or jaws. I have adopted its application for the last thirty years with complete success, never having used or countenanced the exhibition of chloroform, ether, or nitrous oxide gas for this *minor* surgical operation. The benumbing, or *mechanical anæsthesia,* of the temporal branches of nerves obtunds the whole nerve to a sufficient extent to allow the teeth to be removed with sensation so slight, which, if not attending a special surgical operation, would scarcely be noticed by the patient. One of two modes may be adopted. Application of ice to the temples, which is somewhat distressing, the sensation of cold striking deeply. The other, to which I give the preference, is done by an assistant, with each of his middle fingers pressing their points (of the fingers) with persistent firmness and force into the *fossa* or hollow behind the ridge of the temporal bone, which forms the external bone

PLATE I.

ORIGIN AND DISTRIBUTION OF THE GREAT FIFTH PAIR OF NERVES.

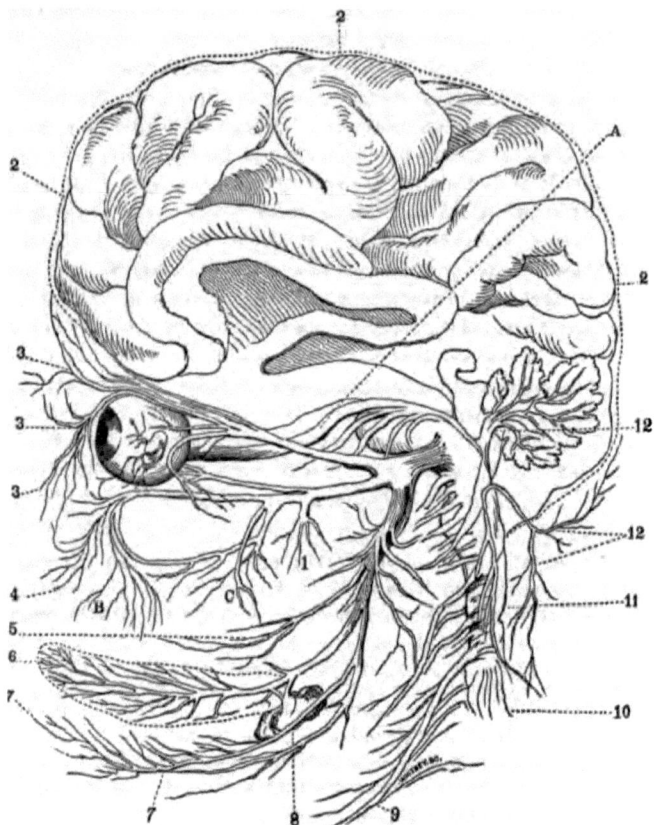

EXPLANATION OF PLATE I.

This plate represents a section of the brain showing the origin of the great fifth pair of nerves, or GRAND SENSITIVE NERVE OF THE HEAD AND MOTOR OF THE JAWS, and the distribution of their principal branches, the sentient points of which are the sympathetic points where dento-neuralgic symptoms (or pain) are experienced, and which, to a limited extent, are more detailed by the nervous branches distributed. (See Plates II. and III.)

A. The optic nerve. Nerve of vision.

B. The anterior or front nerve branches of the second branch of the fifth pair of nerves supplying the right side front teeth.

C. The posterior or back branches of the same branch of the fifth pair, supplying the back teeth, including the wisdom teeth.

circle orbit of the eye. Pressure for one minute is all that is necessary. The practice is as simple as it is harmless, and leaves no after unpleasant sensation to annoy the patient. It is an instinctive method often adopted by people themselves, who press their temples with their fingers to relieve themselves temporarily of the acute paroxysms of nervous headache. This temporary pressure, with sufficient force, is all that is required to remove teeth painlessly. Moreover, it obviates the danger attending the administering of chloroform, ether, laughing gas, etc. by ignorant, clinic-educated, "accomplished" (!) dentists, such as Dr. Daboll (M.D. !) describes, who attend dental clinics, but never attend school. Read what a circular says, thrown into my *sanctum* as I am writing, asking for my patronage. It is over a name with the initials D.D.S. added thereto, which, in this instance, certainly must mean DOCTOR OF DENTAL STUPIDITY, or worse. "LAUGHING GAS FOR THE NERVOUS AND DELICATE." "In the past three years," says the circular,

---

Fig. 1. The palatine nerves of the same second branch, supplying the muscles of the palatine arch, tonsils, etc.

Figs 2, 2, 2. The strong membrane inclosing the brain, the dura mater.

Figs. 3, 3, 3. The first great branch of the fifth pair giving off the OPHTHALMIC branch of nerves, the frontal, or supraorbital, the nasal, and the lachrymal nerves.

Fig. 4. The nerves of the lip from the second branch of the fifth pair, or great maxillary nerve of the upper teeth. These nerves anastomose—mix with and join—with the seventh pair of nerves.

Fig. 5. Linguo-amygdaline and pharyngeal nerve of the great third branch of the fifth pair of nerves.

Fig. 6. The gustatory nerve of taste descending to the tongue; it is joined by a branch of the *chorda tympani* nerve, and unites with the *portio dura* of the seventh pair of nerves as it is passing through the ear. The gustatory nerve sends off twigs to the salivary glands and muscles situated betwixt the jaw-bone and tongue, and finally communicates with the ninth pair of nerves, which we find has connection with the eighth pair of nerves, with the spinal, accessory, and sympathetic, the cervical and phrenic nerves.

Figs. 7, 7. The lower maxillary nerve as it passes through the lower jaw-bone giving off twigs to the teeth, and then emerging from the *mental hole*, dividing into two branches, and distributing their fibrils to the chin, lower lip, throat, etc. The sublingual gland.

Figs. 9, 10, 11, 12. The tenth, eleventh, and twelfth pairs present the suboccipital nerves and the four cervical nerves. High in the neck and under the jaw they are connected with the *portio dura* of the seventh pair, and with the fifth pair, the *dental nerves*, and with the eighth and ninth pairs. The fourth cervical nerves, fig. 10, with the third cervical nerves, fig. 9, and fifth cervical nerves, not illustrated on the map, form the origin of the PHRENIC NERVE of the diaphragm, an important organ of *respiration*. These anastomose (connect) with the other cervical nerves and first dorsal nerves, forming the brachial or intricate AXILLARY PLEXUS of nerves, which extend to the arm, forearm, hand, and fingers.

PLATE II.

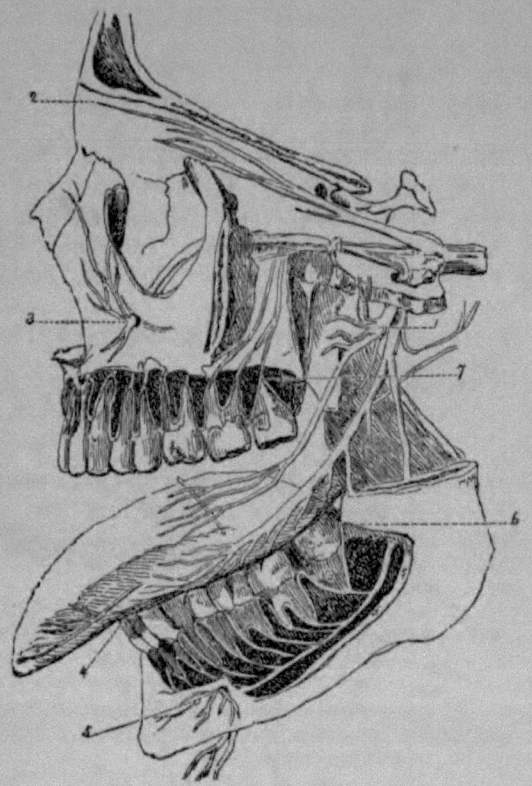

Explanation of Plate II.

Fig. 1. Post musculi-alveoli nerve.

Fig. 2. The frontal or supraorbital nerve passing from the superciliary foramen and spreading over the forehead.

Fig. 3. The facial nerve as it emerges from the infraorbital foramen, after having given off twigs to each tooth of the upper jaw.

Fig. 4. The gustatory nerve—nerve of taste passing along the side of the tongue.

Fig. 5. The lower maxillary nerve emerging from the mental foramen of the jaw-bone, after having given off twigs to each of the lower teeth.

Figs. 6, 7. The lower and upper wisdom teeth.

PLATE III.

THE SUPERFICIAL DISTRIBUTION OF THE LARGER BRANCHES OF THE FIFTH,
AND PORTION OF THE SEVENTH, IN CONNECTION WITH THE NERVES OF THE
NECK AND THROAT.

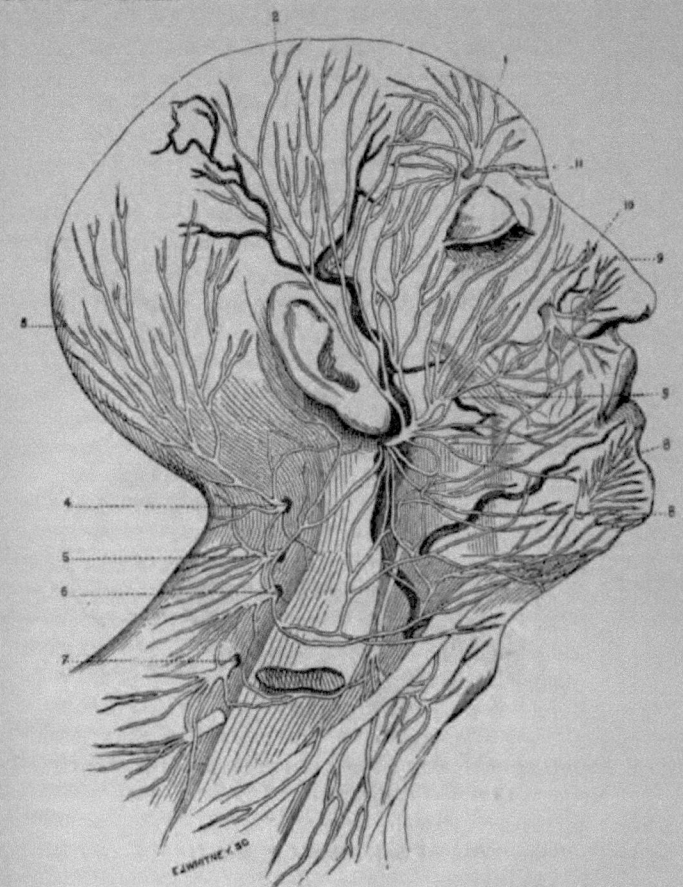

EXPLANATION OF PLATE III.

Figs. 1, 11. The frontal nerve and branches distributed over the forehead.

Figs. 2, 9. The great transverse or temporal, parietal and facial distribution of
the seventh pair of nerves, and their connecting or anastomosing with the fifth
pair of nerves.

Fig. 3. The distribution of the occipital nerve over the back part of the head.

Figs. 4, 5, 6, 7. The neck—cervical—nerves and their connecting branches
which lead to the arm, forearm, hands, and fingers.

Figs. 8, 8. The mental nerve spreading over the forepart of the throat, over
the chin, lower lip, and finally joining the nerves of the face, etc.

"I have administered the *gas* to persons afflicted (!) (AFFLICTED is a good word) with *heart* and *lung* diseases, and many of them in very delicate health." It would be a queer phenomenon to find *heart* and *lung* diseased persons in a robust state of health. Two deaths have occurred in dental offices in this city within the last three years, the victims of heart and lung disease, but prematurely finished off by "laughing gas." Upon one an inquest was held; the other was "hushed up." We remember the cry of "Free trade and sailors' rights," but here we have a D.D.S.—heaven save the mark!—in defiance of all legal, moral, and medico-physical laws and science, advertising his peculiar merits to perpetrate this *grave* offense upon the ignorance and credulity of "an enlightened public," and upon diseased, harmless patients; yet in all scientific gravity he asks *medical men* to patronize his peculiar specialty.

I need not enlarge upon the importance, nor recapitulate the offices of the grand sensitive nerve of the head. It is only necessary to remind the reader that the fifth pair of nerves goes everywhere, to the head and face externally and internally; that it is universally the nerve of common sensibility; that it possesses the peculiar *gustatory* sensibility of this nerve-branch; that it gives sensibility to the surface of the eye; and that it is the nerve of the muscles of the jaw.

Of the whole nervous system, perhaps there is no other nerve thought less about, or more trifled with, irritated, or treated more recklessly. This great sensitive nerve appears to be the foot-ball of every broken-down tradesman who "gets up a new infallible hair restorative and hair dye" made of *paralyzing* poisons; of every simpleton who thinks eyes without "*speculation*" (expression) in them is beauty, and who poisons them with *belladonna ;* of every hair-bleaching barber; of every tag-rag, bob-tail artisan, etc. who, as a *dernier ressort*, takes up the art of dentistry, and attends *dental clinics* to obtain a *modicum* of knowledge with which to present himself as a professor of dentistry in his own office, where, with reckless ignorance and with Sir Oracle importance, he poisons nerves with arsenic, aconite, chloride of zinc, etc., without a particle of knowledge of any difference in their character or of their appropriate application; while he "destroys nerves" as if they were so many rats hidden in holes; or, at a venture, he extracts every good tooth to replace them with what he terms a "new denture."

I may be permitted here to remark upon the grave error and injury being done to the character and progress of the dental profession by what is termed "*dental clinics*." For very many years we have had well-established DENTAL COLLEGES in PHILADELPHIA and BALTIMORE, with other schools of lesser note, where the honest dental student, devoting his time, his money, and application to his collegiate studies, can and does acquire all the preliminary learning, theory, and practical knowledge necessary to form a substantial basis upon which to build his future professional progress and reputation.

Many young gentlemen, imbued with this laudable and exalted ambition, avail themselves of these opportunities and advantages. After years of zealous toil, in the full faith that they have alike done justice to themselves, as well as to their intentions of doing the same to the character of the profession they have selected, and to those who may confide in their professional capacity, knowledge, and abilities to serve them, what do they find as their reward for their sacrifice of time, money, and application? What is the incentive to others to follow their scrupulous example? Their reward is to find, after all their sacrifices,— for sacrifice it is under the present system,—that a certain number of ORACLES "get up dental clinics" in the highways and in public places, and there invite tag-rag and bob-tail dentists *par excellence*, who have not the slightest claim upon them or the profession, who have never matriculated, and who have never been to school, to come and see how *they* fill teeth. This is the Alpha and Omega of their clinics. We never find these "clinics" filling the teeth of the *cachectic*, the *anæmic*, and the *nervous*. No, the patients are iron-jawed gentlemen "without nerves," that can sit still and keep open their mouths for hours together, and have their teeth sledge-hammered all the time without wincing,—to say nothing of the superabundance of eager assistants to aid the success of the operations. The clinical student and the self-graduated dentist, who has never expended a moment to study or a penny to attend a dental school, who jumps from a fishmonger's stand or from a dry goods yard measure, is your "cheap dentist;" he poisons teeth with arsenic, aconite, and chloride of zinc, and poisons the jaws and nerves too. He administers nitrous oxide, or laughing-gas, "free," "gratis," "for nothing," warranted better prepared and more pure than can be found in any other shop. He wears diamond studs, perfumes his hands, pomades his hair, and travels upon his beard and handsome person, *i.e.* shirt front, while the professional dental student starves, or becomes "*assistant*" to some successful ignoramus, or is exiled from his home. Thus dental clinics are PROFESSIONAL DESTRUCTIVES. They not only do a gross injustice to our dental schools, but to the oracles themselves, who make themselves public *peripatetic* teachers in profitless but injurious competition with our dental colleges. COLLEGIATE CLINICS are not only right, but they are due to *matriculated students*, and to them alone— not to outsiders.

My "Notes," etc., for a Memoir on the Pathology of the Teeth, may not be acceptable—pleasing—to all the profession as it is constituted. But they will be recognized by those actuated with the desire—as I am—of seeing the profession in its proper position and enjoying its proper status in public estimation, and by the faculty, with the other specialties of the healing art. To attain this end, I claim to be influenced by the highest professional feeling. In speaking and demonstrating the truth, therefore, I do not court applause, nor do I expect any profit for speaking the truth; at the same time I do not fear to meet the frowns of any man for doing so. If my "Notes" do not stand the test of scrutiny, my wish is to have them disregarded and exploded, as the imaginations of a visionary. But, on the contrary, if they rest—as my experience tells me they do—on the immutability of truth, it behoves every dentist, every lover of his profession, and every medical practitioner, to award them that weight and consideration which their importance demand, and by *their* additional experience and observations to continue the work until it shall be demonstrated perfectly.